"I've had just about enough of you."

Max spoke with such contempt that Cairo winced. "I've met your type before. You think that, just because you've got money and smart clothes, all you have to do is crook your finger, and everyone and everything will fall at your feet. Well the desert's not like that, and nor am I. Neither of us is for sale. So you may as well go back to the city where you belong, and learn to take no for an answer!"

Jessica Hart had a varied career before she began writing for Harlequin Romance. She worked as a waitress, a theater production assistant, an outback cook, a news-desk secretary and an English teacher—as she traveled around the world to such places as Egypt, Kenya, Jakarta and Australia. She now lives in the north of England, where she is studying for a history degree.

Books by Jessica Hart

HARLEQUIN ROMANCE
3213—THE TROUBLE WITH LOVE
3231—WOMAN AT WILLAGONG CREEK
3302—THE BECKONING FLAME
3334—A SENSIBLE WIFE

OASIS OF
THE HEART
Jessica Hart

Harlequin Books

TORONTO • NEW YORK • LONDON
AMSTERDAM • PARIS • SYDNEY • HAMBURG
STOCKHOLM • ATHENS • TOKYO • MILAN
MADRID • WARSAW • BUDAPEST • AUCKLAND

ISBN 0-373-17232-X

OASIS OF THE HEART

Copyright © 1993 by Jessica Hart.

First North American Publication 1995.

Printed in U.S.A.

CHAPTER ONE

'MAX FALCONER? You're in luck. That's him over there.'

Cairo's gaze followed the pointing finger to where a lean, dusty-looking man was unloading equipment from the back of an equally dusty pick-up truck. Unaware of her interest, he paused to take off his hat and wipe his forehead with the back of his arm in a gesture that told Cairo that he was as hot and tired as she was.

Her green eyes rested on him a little doubtfully. Max Falconer will help you, they had all said. You couldn't have a better guide, they'd told her. Max knows his way around the plateau as well as any Tuareg.

Cairo had been intrigued by what she had been told of the Englishman who had made his home in the desert, and had secretly imagined a flamboyant, rather romantic figure, but as she watched him methodically unload his truck she was conscious of a pang of disappointment. This man wasn't romantic at all. He merely looked tired and bad-tempered.

'Are you sure that's him?' she asked the young engineer who had stopped to give her directions.

He grinned. 'That's him all right. There's only one Max Falconer.'

Cairo suppressed a sigh. Nothing was turning out as she had expected this trip. There were no guides available in the town, but when she had been told about the English geologist her spirits had risen once more. It would be even better if she had a friendly, English-speaking companion for the trip, especially if he was as interesting as he had been made out to be. Now, her green eyes were unimpressed as she studied the real Max Falconer. He was very far from being the flamboyant figure she had envisaged. In fact, she couldn't imagine anyone looking *less* flamboyant. There was an austere, contained air about him, a sense of deliberate self-control, and, although she had to acknowledge that he looked more than competent, he certainly didn't look very friendly. He had very ordinary-looking brown hair, and what she could see of his face held a guarded expression. Cairo's hopes for a fascinating guide and congenial companion were fading rapidly.

Still, beggars couldn't be choosers, she reminded herself. She *had* to get up that plateau, and, if Max Falconer was the only person who could take her there, then she would just have to put up with him.

Squaring her shoulders, she smiled her thanks and began to pick her way across the grit and rubble towards Max. The engineer watched her go with regret. Cool, beautiful girls were a rare sight in the rough and ready surroundings of a desert construction camp, and his eyes rested appreciatively on the long, slim legs shimmering in the heat haze as she approached the pick-up truck.

In spite of appearances, Cairo was feeling anything but cool. The heat was crushing and the harsh desert sunlight seemed to bounce around her, glancing off her bright hair like metal. For the umpteenth time, she wished she were at home in a wet and windy London spring. She'd been told that Max Falconer had been in Shofrar for years, that he actually *chose* to live here. Cairo couldn't imagine anyone wanting to live in this brown, barren furnace of a country. As far as she could see, there was nothing here but a few rocks, a chaotic bureaucracy and mile upon mile of flat, featureless desert.

Thinking wistfully of elegant city streets as she walked down the dusty road, Cairo had momentarily forgotten about Max until she suddenly realised that he had straightened and was watching her approach. Through the heat, her gaze met his, and she faltered.

His eyes were intensely light in his sunburnt face, so icy and unexpected that she had to resist the urge to step backwards. She couldn't tell what colour they were. She only knew that they were very cold and chillingly indifferent, and that they made her heart lurch uncomfortably.

Max turned back to the truck, releasing her from that glacial look, and Cairo took a sharp, involuntary breath. She felt oddly shaken. There was something in his eyes that forced her to rearrange her ideas about him yet again. The severity she had noticed from a distance hid an aura of suppressed power that was unmistakable at close quarters. This was no dully capable geologist. This man was tough, and far from unimpressive.

She had been right about the bad temper though. His brows were drawn together over his nose and his mouth was set in a grim line. After that one look, he had ignored her, and something about the deliberate way he went on unloading the vehicle made Cairo's hackles rise.

'Are you Max Falconer?' Her voice came out much sharper than she intended. She had been thrown off balance by the unexpected impact of his eyes, but it was only because they were so light in his dark face, she reasoned. She certainly wasn't going to let herself be intimidated by *that*!

Max hoisted a battered metal box off the back and set it carefully on the ground before he answered. 'Presumably Chris has just told you who I am, or he wouldn't have pointed me out.' It was strange that a voice so deep and deliberate could sound so cold. 'Why bother to ask him if you're not going to believe him?'

'Why not just say yes or no?' Cairo retorted with a snap. It had been a long day. She was hot and tired and fed up with trekking around Menesset in search of a man who was turning out to be thoroughly disagreeable. If only she didn't have to ask a favour of him!

Taking a deep breath, she took off her sunglasses so that he could see who he was talking to, and forced herself to sound pleasant. 'My name's Cairo Kingswood.' Her eyes were screwed up against the glare, but she saw his gaze flick up at her, narrowed and uncomfortably penetrating, before it dropped back to the dusty truck. Something tugged at the back of Cairo's mind, something that might have been recognition, but she brushed the thought away irritably. She was sure she would have remembered if she had ever met anyone as rude as Max Falconer before! Look at him, carrying on stacking up his wretched boxes as if she wasn't there! He hadn't even acknowledged her introduction.

'I've got a bit of a problem,' she said at last, when it was obvious he wasn't going to say anything. 'Everyone tells me that you're the one person who can help me.'

Max lifted the last box off the truck, and banged the tailgate back up. Brushing his hands on his khaki trousers, he looked at Cairo at last. 'Who's *everyone*?' His eyes, she saw now, were a pale grey-green, their startling lightness intensified by a fringe of dark, almost sooty lashes.

'Just about everyone I've talked to since I arrived in Shofrar yesterday,' said Cairo, forcing her mind away from his eyes and back to the problem in hand. She thought morosely of her frustrating morning trailing around Menesset, of endless shaking heads and charming shrugs of regret and the last word of advice: find Max Falconer. Now she had found him, and suddenly her request didn't seem quite so simple.

She hesitated for a moment, then pointed with her sunglasses towards the vast, steep-sided plateau that reared out of the flat desert in the distance. From the camp on the outskirts of Menesset, it appeared a vast table of rock, but she knew that it stretched for hundreds of miles, its stony surface eroded by unimaginable time into a weird moonscape. The plateau was about as far from civilisation as you could get, and Cairo shuddered at the very thought of it, but that was where she had to go. 'I need a guide to take me up there,' she said.

'Plenty of guides in Menesset,' Max said unhelpfully.

'But there aren't.' Cairo's hair was dark, shining gold, and fell in soft waves to her jaw. Now she pushed it away from her face in frustration. 'I didn't take into account that Shofrar is a Muslim country. Ramadan ends tonight so everyone's celebrating Id-el-Fitr and no one's going anywhere for the next few days. I haven't got long, and I can't afford to wait for them all to come back from their holidays.'

Max was unsympathetic. 'You should have thought of that before you came,' he said, opening the door of the pick-up and leaning inside to collect a notebook from the dashboard. 'It doesn't take much to find out when the local holidays are before you leave, and if you'd bothered to do that much research you'd have found out that this is no time to be in the desert anyway. It's much too hot to climb the plateau now. The tourist season ended a month ago.'

'I was told you go up to the plateau all the time,' Cairo protested as he straightened.

'I do—but I'm not a tourist.'

'Nor am I,' she said. 'I'm here on business.'

'Business?' he echoed incredulously, staring at her with that unnervingly light gaze. 'How can you possibly have business on the plateau?'

'I'm here to represent my clients, Haydn Deane Associates,' said Cairo, trying to sound professional, but the effect was rather spoiled by having her face screwed up against the sun. To hell with courtesy, she thought as she put the sunglasses back on her nose. It was wasted on Max anyway. The dark glasses made her feel cooler and more businesslike. 'Haydn Deane are an advertising company,' she went on. 'They're anxious to do a fashion shoot using the plateau as a backdrop.'

To her chagrin, instead of being impressed as he was meant to be, Max Falconer burst out laughing. 'A fashion shoot on the plateau? They must be mad!' His teeth were strong and white and the laughter momentarily dissolved the grimly austere lines of his face.

'Haydn Deane are very far from mad,' Cairo said coldly, insulted and more than a little disconcerted by the way his laugh transformed his face. 'They're a creative and extremely successful company who are responsible for a number of award-winning advertisements.'

'They'll be responsible for an award-winning cock-up if they try and do a shoot here,' said Max brutally. He had stopped laughing and she decided she must have imagined that glimpse of a suddenly attractive man. 'They've got no idea what it's like.'

Cairo struggled to keep her cool. She mustn't lose her temper now! 'That's precisely why I'm here. My partner and I run a consultancy doing all the liaison and preparatory work on one-off international projects like this. Far from having ''no idea'', our clients are so well aware of the likely problems that they have employed me to do a reconnaissance of possible sites and iron out all the logistical problems before they arrive. Surely that makes sense?' she added with artificial sweetness, but Max was unmoved.

He pushed his notebook into the pocket of his old blue shirt. It was very faded and had an oil stain on one sleeve, and his trousers weren't in much better condition. 'If you think it makes sense to take a group of self-styled creative city people into one of the hottest and most inhospitable places of the world in the middle of summer, you must be out of your mind!'

'The end of May isn't summer,' said Cairo stubbornly. 'I know it will be hot, but I've been told it's quite possible.'

'It's possible if you're very fit, very tough and have a good guide. You, Miss Kingswood, don't seem to fit into any of those categories.'

Cairo lifted her chin. 'I'm tougher than I look.'

'I'm sure you're quite tough enough when it comes to getting your own way,' said Max, looking her up and down, his cold eyes assessing her smooth skin, the thick,

glinting hair and effortlessly elegant clothes. She wore
a knee-length linen skirt with low-heeled pumps and a
silky olive-green shirt. 'I've met your type before,' he
said in a hard voice. 'You look like a spoilt brat to me.
I don't suppose you've ever done a day's work in your
life, let alone had to rough it.'

This was uncomfortably close to the truth and Cairo's
eyes slid away from his, her jaw working in frustration.
She was tired of being dismissed as spoilt by people who
never made the effort to know her any better. It wasn't
her fault that her father had pampered and indulged her
from the day she was born, and, if she hadn't had any
experience of work before now, well, that had all had
to change. It had taken long enough for anyone to give
her the chance to do a day's work! Only Piers had been
prepared to give her a chance, and the thought of her
partner and why she was here stiffened her resolve.

'I'm working now,' she told Max and glanced dis-
dainfully around her at the stark prefabricated buildings
of the camp and the dusty road which stretched off towards the empty horizon. 'I can assure you, I'm not
here for the fun of it! I've got a job to do up on the
plateau, and I've done plenty of research about what's
involved.'

'If you'd done any research at all, you'd have known
there's no way you could get an advertising team up
there.' Max gestured towards the plateau, which seemed
to float above the heat along the distant horizon. 'Did
you find out how long it takes to climb up to? Eleven
hours, and that's on a good day. Eleven hours of
climbing an almost vertical path in temperatures of well
over a hundred degrees, and you can't stop and rest for
too long, or you'd never get to the top before dark. And
the plateau is not a place to be wandering around in the
dark, Cairo Kingswood. It's full of treacherous crevices
and gulleys. If you fall down them, you never get up
again.' Max glanced at her appalled expression and shook

his head. 'You wouldn't last five minutes,' he said with finality.

'Want a bet?' said Cairo, much more bravely than she felt.

'No, because it's not going to be put to the test,' he said with flat refusal. He retrieved a battered hat from the cab, brushed the dust off it and set it on his head. 'I'm not prepared to take you up to the plateau, and that's that.'

Cairo took a deep breath. He couldn't refuse, not after it had taken all this time just to find him! She tried an appealing smile. 'Please,' she begged, even though it went against the grain to be grovelling to him. 'It's very important.'

'What's important about advertising?' Max looked at her with a contemptuous expression. 'The whole business is corrupt. All advertising does is sell false images to persuade people to spend their money on things they don't need and probably don't even want. As far as I'm concerned, that's dishonest, not *important*!'

Cairo bit her lip, taken aback by the unexpected bitterness in his voice. Why should he care so much about advertising? It could hardly affect him much stuck out here! 'It's important to me to do my job,' she said after a moment. 'I can't do that unless I get up on to the plateau, and you're the only person who can take me.'

'My heart bleeds for you,' he said shortly, shutting the door of the cab, and Cairo's heart seethed at his indifference.

He could have shown a little more concern at her plight! What was she to do now? She couldn't go home and tell Haydn Deane she hadn't been able to get up on to the plateau. Piers was relying on her to make a success of this, their first job, and she couldn't let him down. If word got round that they were unreliable, they would never get any more work, she thought desperately, and what would happen to her father then?

She watched helplessly as he bent to secure the lid on one of the boxes. 'Won't you change your mind?' she asked, hating herself for the pleading note in her voice.

'Why should I?' Max asked, straightening abruptly, and at the expression on his face Cairo took an involuntary step backwards. 'You don't impress me with all your talk of business and award-winning advertisers.' His voice was scathing and she felt herself flush humiliatingly. 'As far as I'm concerned, if we had no advertisers, the world would be a far better place, and if you think I'm going to waste my time on a totally irresponsible venture like the one you've described to me, just to indulge some brainless executive's ego, you've got another think coming. Do I make myself clear?'

'Perfectly,' said Cairo in a frosty voice. She wasn't used to being talked to like that, and she didn't like it. 'If that's the case, I won't bother you any more.'

'Please don't,' said Max.

He really was insufferable! Turning on her heel, Cairo stalked back along the road to the guest quarters and slammed the door of her room behind her. She wished she had never heard of Haydn Deane or Shofrar, wished Piers had never talked her into coming here. The place was a nightmare and the bureaucracy even worse, and to cap it all she had had to end up pleading with the likes of Max Falconer.

Cairo banged around the room furiously. What did he have to feel so superior about, anyway? He was only some grubby geologist.

Her eyes ached from the glare outside and she washed her face with cold water. The confrontation with Max Falconer had left her tense and frustrated, and her angry face glared back at her from the mirror above the basin, cheeks flushed and slanting green eyes a-glitter.

Turning up the air-conditioning, she threw herself down on the narrow bed with a sigh. 'There's nothing to it,' Piers had said. 'All you've got to do is get yourself up on to that plateau, find a couple of good locations and then fix up a few donkeys to take everyone up there next month. It'll be easy.'

Easy? Cairo grimaced at the ceiling. It hadn't taken long to find out that things were going to be far from easy. She would have to wade through interminable red tape to get all the necessary permits from the government, and that was nothing compared to the problem of getting on to the plateau in the first place. If only she had arrived a week earlier, she could have found a guide in Menesset and been up and down the plateau long before the holiday, instead of being reduced to grovelling to Max Falconer—and much good that had done her!

Why couldn't Haydn Deane have chosen somewhere a little more accessible for the shoot? Max was right, she admitted grudgingly. Some bright spark had probably seen some pictures of the plateau and decided that it would make a suitably dramatic location without giving any thought to how they were going to get all the people and equipment required up there.

'That's where we come in,' Piers had said excitedly. 'Once they realised how difficult it was going to be, they were only too glad to let us take care of all the arrangements for them.'

He threw himself down at his desk and looked over it at Cairo, who was still reeling from the shock of finding that she was to be sent off into the middle of the Sahara. 'What's the matter? This is the break we've been waiting for, Cairo! If we make a success of this job, word will get around, and we'll just take off. They'll be beating a path to our door in no time.'

'Why do I have to go?' she demanded. When they had first set up their consultancy, they had planned to operate in European cities, not in the wilds of North Africa. Cairo didn't know anything about deserts, other than the fact that she was sure she never wanted to see one.

Piers waved a casual hand. 'It has to be someone who speaks French so they can deal with the government officials.'

'You speak French,' she pointed out, unimpressed.

'Not as well as you. Besides...' Piers hesitated, and fiddled with his pen '...they particularly asked for you.'

'For *me*? Why me?'

Her partner couldn't quite meet her eyes. 'They thought your Middle Eastern experience would come in useful in a place like Shofrar.'

'My *what*?' Cairo gaped at him, and Piers had the grace to blush. Haydn Deane, it turned out, had been intrigued by Cairo's unusual name when Piers had first approached them, and he had been quick to capitalise on their interest by embroidering the truth about her experience.

Cairo was horrified. 'Piers, being born in Egypt and spending five years in Bahrain as a child hardly qualifies me as an expert on the Middle East! And even if it did, Shofrar is in North Africa, in case you haven't looked at a map recently.'

'Haydn Deane don't care about that,' said Piers, on the defensive. 'All they care about is getting the arrangements for the shoot fixed up. What difference does it make? I know that you can do the job with or without any experience, and the important thing was to get the contract.'

'It doesn't sound very ethical to me,' said Cairo stringently. 'In fact, it sounds remarkably like lying.'

'You'd never guess that a girl who looks as sophisticated as you do could have such old-fashioned ideas,' Piers grumbled. 'Sometimes I think an uncomfortably puritanical heart lies beneath that glamorous image of yours.' When Cairo still looked mutinous, he leaned forward persuasively. 'Look, you can't let stupid principles stand in the way of us getting this contract. If you're going to turn down opportunities like this, you might as well go back to waitressing, and you'll never pay your father's debts off that way, will you?'

It was an unkind shot, and Cairo's lips tightened, but she knew that Piers was right. Her father was depending on her now.

'It'll be easy,' Piers went on confidently. 'If this contract goes well, we'll be able to repay your godmother the money she lent you to get started, and then we'll start raking in the profits, you wait and see. All you've got to do is get yourself up that plateau.'

How?

Cairo hoisted herself upright now, propped the pillow up behind her and leant back against the wall with a sigh. She had to think. There must be some way she could get up the plateau. She could live with disappointing Piers and Haydn Deane, but she couldn't let her father down. For the first twenty-five years of her life, he had given her everything, and now it was her turn to do what she could for him.

In her mind, she went over her conversation with Max Falconer again. Perhaps she had just approached him the wrong way? She had been hot and tired and cross, and so had he. Thrown off balance by those piercing eyes, she had probably been more brittle than she intended, Cairo decided. He might not have understood that she was offering him a business deal. Money hadn't been mentioned; he might well have thought that she was asking him to take her up as a favour.

That was it! Cairo sat bolt upright, convinced that she had found the reason for Max's hostility. She would talk to him again tonight, when they were both in a better mood, and explain that she was fully prepared to pay for his services. Judging by his shabby clothes and battered old truck, he might welcome some extra cash.

Confidence restored, Cairo swung her legs off the bed and rummaged in her suitcase for her most flattering outfit. She would pull out all the stops this evening, and Max would be so bowled over by her charm that he wouldn't be able to resist coming to a deal! Cairo had a momentary qualm as she hung up her black dress and tried to imagine Max Falconer being bowled over, but she shrugged it aside. After a shower and a beer, he would be much more approachable. He might even apologise for being so unhelpful...

It was lucky that she had been able to stay at the camp, Cairo decided as she washed her hair, remembering the primitive hotel in Menesset with a shudder. If she hadn't met Bruce Mitchell she could be there now. Bruce was the administration manager of the huge construction camp some ten miles from Menesset, and it was he who had told her where she might find Max.

'He comes and goes as he pleases, but he's based at the camp with the rest of us, so you've a better chance of finding him there than anywhere,' he had said. 'Why don't you come back with me? We've some guest rooms that don't get used much in the hot season, so you could stay there until Max turns up. It's not very grand—just a bar and a mess where all the unmarried men eat—but I know they'll all be delighted at the prospect of some female company for a change.'

Max Falconer hadn't seemed very delighted, Cairo remembered as she wriggled into her dress. Smoothing it down over her hips, she studied her reflection critically and wondered what he would think. Her face was so familiar to her that she normally gave it little thought, but tonight she leaned closer to the mirror and stared at herself as if she had never seen it before, trying to see herself through Max's eyes. She had an unusual, triangular face, with a wide jaw and high cheekbones, and green eyes slanting like a cat's below winged brows. Her thick, waving blonde hair was bluntly cut to the jawline. It was a memorable face, she decided. Max might not have liked her, but he would recognise her when he met her again, and, at the thought, she remembered with some puzzlement that moment when she could have sworn that she had met Max before. He wasn't the forgettable type either.

His image rose before her, peculiarly vivid. She could picture those startlingly light eyes with absolute clarity, could have drawn exactly the line of his mouth and the angle of his cheekbones. Without quite knowing why, Cairo shivered.

The dress was one of her favourites, left over, like all her clothes, from the good days before the easy, luxurious world her father had built for her had fallen about her ears. Exquisitely cut, the soft black material flattered the soft curves of her body and gave her skin a luminous glow. In spite of its demure design, it was an undeniably sexy dress, and always made Cairo feel good when she wore it.

Would Max think it was sexy? Unaccountably, Cairo felt a blush steal up her throat at the thought of his eyes upon her. In the normal course of events, she would never even have noticed him, she told herself. There was nothing special about him, except for those light eyes that looked through you, and that quality of tightly coiled strength. He had no warmth, no charm, nothing to recommend him at all. She wouldn't care a bit about what he thought if it hadn't been for the fact that she wanted to charm him into doing what she wanted. That was what she convinced herself, anyway.

When Bruce Mitchell took Cairo into the bar that night, there was a brief, stunned silence as seventy-five pairs of male eyes took in the vision standing in the doorway. Used to admiration, Cairo took it all in her stride, but was annoyed to find her own gaze straying round the room in search of Max.

She spotted him eventually, leaning against the bar at the far end, and her heart gave an uncomfortable jolt. He was half turned away from her, and, even though he was surrounded by tough-looking men, Cairo couldn't help noticing how distinctive he was. It wasn't anything to do with how he looked; there were plenty of lean, rangy-looking men around with deep tans and dark brown hair, but there was a cool air of self-containment about Max that set him apart. He didn't smile very often, but whenever he did his smile caught at the edge of her eye and her gaze would flicker over towards him.

If Max was aware of her presence in the bar, he gave no sign of it, and Cairo couldn't help feeling rather put out. She knew quite well that she was a very attractive girl, and just about every other man in the place was eyeing her with appreciation, but Max didn't even seem to have noticed she was there at all.

The longer his shoulder remained resolutely turned towards her, the more determined Cairo became to attract his attention. She smiled and laughed and chatted animatedly, gathering a cluster of admiring men around her, but no matter how many times she glanced over at Max he continued to ignore her. Cairo's green eyes began to take on a frustrated glitter. How could she charm him if he wouldn't even notice her?

'How did you get on with Max?' Bruce asked her as they went into the mess for dinner. 'Is he going to take you up with him tomorrow morning?'

'Tomorrow morning?'

'Yes, he told me he was going straight back up on to the plateau. Usually he stays here for a couple of days, but I wondered if it might have been because you wanted to go up as soon as possible.'

It was far more likely that he was going back to get out of her way, Cairo reflected, but there was no point in telling Bruce just how disastrous her confrontation with Max had been.

'We haven't finalised the details yet,' she said vaguely. 'I can't quite remember where he said he would be setting off from.'

'Probably up by Oued Misra.' Bruce was as helpful as she had hoped. 'The quickest path leaves from there, and I know Max usually goes that way. He sends his supplies up by donkey, and they go by an easier but much longer route, but I wouldn't have thought he'd take you that way.'

Cairo's brain was ticking furiously. 'Does it take long to get to Oued Misra from here?' she asked artlessly.

'About forty minutes in a car. Max gets one of the drivers to drop him off, so no doubt he'll take you with him.'

Cairo ate her meal thoughtfully, her mind working busily on contingency plans. Her best bet was still to persuade Max to think again, she decided. If he wasn't going to do what any normal man would have done and come over and say hello, she would just have to go over to him. There was no sign of him in the mess, but when they went back to the bar she caught sight of a lean, compact figure heading towards the door, and, murmuring an excuse to Bruce, she hurried after him.

The door swung to behind her as she stepped out into the night. Max was standing a few feet away, hands dug into his trouser pockets, staring down at the ground as if in deep thought. The light from the mess windows caught one side of his face, highlighting the strong cheekbones and the decisive line of his jaw. A weird sense of *déjà vu* swept over Cairo without warning, and she hesitated, caught off balance by the sudden certainty that she had come up behind Max like this some time before.

Probably a trick of the brain, Cairo told herself. She had read somewhere about the effect being cause by nerve messages to the brain getting ahead of themselves. At least that would explain why she should feel there was something familiar about a man she could swear she had never met before in her life. It wasn't just a case of not remembering his face. She couldn't even imagine a place where she *might* have come across anyone as different as Max Falconer. He was English, of course, but that was absolutely all they had in common. No, she couldn't have met him before. She was sure of that.

Still, it was a strangely unsettling feeling, and Cairo made a deliberate effort to shrug it aside as she stepped forward. 'Hello,' she said.

Max's head jerked up, but he didn't respond to her greeting. Instead he watched her silently, with eyes that were shadowed and unreadable in the darkness.

'I was hoping to see you this evening,' she said after a moment. His grimly silent presence was unnerving.

'Why?'

Cairo suppressed a sigh. Couldn't he at least *try* to be pleasant? She tried a charming smile. It had left Bruce Mitchell and half the men in the mess looking dazed, but won absolutely no response from Max. 'I wanted to apologise,' she persevered. 'I suppose I didn't pick a very good time to pester you this afternoon.'

'There's never a good time to pester me, Miss Kingswood,' Max said discouragingly, and Cairo gritted her teeth.

'I just thought I might not have explained myself very well.'

'I'm not stupid,' he pointed out in a harsh voice. 'I know exactly what you want. You want me to take you up on to the plateau so that you can make plans to bring in a lot of people who want to waste their time and money taking photographs of something people don't need and won't use in a place they won't even recognise.'

Cairo reminded herself of her resolve to be charming, and managed a light laugh. 'That's putting it rather bluntly!'

'It's putting it honestly—not a concept much used in the advertising world, I agree.'

Cairo took a deep breath and tried again. 'I didn't think you hadn't understood what I wanted. I just thought you might not have appreciated that I was proposing a business deal. I'm not asking you to do this for free. I'm quite prepared to pay for your services.'

'The answer is *no*,' said Max, dangerously calm.

'I don't care what it costs,' Cairo said recklessly. 'Are you sure you can afford to give up a chance like this? You could earn more in one trip than the rest of the year.'

As soon as the words were out of her mouth, she knew that she had made a mistake. 'I've had just about enough of you,' said Max with such contempt that she winced. 'I've met your type before. You think that, just because you've got money and smart clothes, all you have to do is crook your finger and everything and everyone will fall at your feet. Well, the desert's not like that, and nor am I. Neither of us is for sale. I wouldn't take you or anyone like you anywhere near the plateau, no matter how much you paid me, so you may as well go back to the city where you belong and learn to take no for an answer!'

CHAPTER TWO

CAIRO shaded her eyes from the glare and watched the car disappear into the distance. When it was no more than a tiny dot smothered in a tell-tale plume of dust, she swallowed. She must be mad!

The silence settled about her like a heavy blanket. Before her, the desert stretched out, flat and brown and empty as far as the horizon and beyond. Behind her loomed the plateau, an intimidating mass of rock that dropped down to the boulder-strewn wasteland where she stood.

Cairo had never felt so alone in her life. Nothing moved. The silence was so absolute that she could hear her heart beating, and, even this early in the morning, the heat was already intense. She turned to look uncertainly up at the plateau to which she had been so determined to climb. The steep, narrow path soon disappeared into a tumble of rocks; she would never be able to find her way by herself.

She would never be able to make it back to camp either, she remembered with a lurch of her stomach. Bruce's driver had been reluctant to leave her here alone, but she had assured him that she had arranged to meet Max and that he needn't wait, terrified that he would hang around until Max appeared and spoil her plan. Now she sat down abruptly on a rock as the enormity of what she had done hit her. She didn't want to think what would happen if Max didn't come.

She didn't really want to think about what would happen if he did, either.

Well, it was too late to change her mind now. Cairo stiffened her spine. She wouldn't have needed to take a risk like this if Max had been more reasonable, she grumbled to herself. If she succumbed to heat exhaustion out here, it would be all his fault. When Max had turned on his heel last night, Cairo had been so angry that her determination to get up to the plateau had hardened to a steely refusal to let him get away with the last word. If he thought he could get the better of Cairo Kingswood with a few sharp words, he was the one who had another think coming! Haydn Deane, Piers, even her father were forgotten. All that mattered was not letting herself be beaten by Max Falconer.

She had lain awake for hours, desperately turning alternatives over in her mind. This plan had occurred to her early on, as soon as Bruce had mentioned where Max began his trek up the plateau, but she had rejected it at first as being too foolhardy. As the night wore on, though, it became clear that if she wanted to get up to the plateau she would have to take the risk.

She had been ready early in the morning and had gone to find Bruce Mitchell's Indian driver as soon as she had established that Max hadn't yet left. The driver had been surprised at her request to drive her to the Oued Misra, but as Bruce had put him at Cairo's disposal he merely shrugged and started the car. Now all Cairo could do was hope that Bruce had been right when he said that Max would leave from here.

If he had decided to go some other way...

'Don't even think about it,' Cairo told herself out loud, jumping to her feet as her voice echoed in the silence. 'Think about Daddy instead.' Her determined face softened as she thought about her father. Her mother had died while she was still a baby and Jeremy Kingswood had cosseted and adored his only child ever since, showering her with presents and every luxury money could buy. It was too late when Cairo had found out that the money wasn't his at all, but she had stood by him through all the scandal and disgrace, knowing that he had done it all for her.

Now it was her turn to look after him. They had sold everything they owned—the cars, the yachts, the houses and apartments, the pictures and antiques were all gone—and Cairo had vowed to pay off what remained of his debts so that they could both start again with a clean slate. If it meant risking her life in the fierce desert sun, well, that was what she would do.

Her eyes ranged the landscape, looking for some sign that she had not made the most appalling mistake, and, in spite of all her bravado, her knees shook with relief when a cloud of dust along the horizon announced the approach of a vehicle. Let it be Max, she prayed as she put her rucksack out of sight and slipped behind the boulder.

Cairo's heart was thumping as she peeked cautiously from her hiding place a few minutes later. It was Max. He was exchanging some joke with the driver as he hoisted his rucksack out of the back of the pick-up truck. His smile lit his face with humour, and, as once before, Cairo found herself thinking irrelevantly that he could be disquietingly attractive when he smiled like that. As Max turned away to dump his pack on the ground, her memory suddenly jolted, but the flash of recognition was gone before she could grasp it. She *had* met him before...but where?

Max was thumping the roof of the cab to let the driver know that he was ready, and as the truck drove off with a cheery wave out of the window and a toot of its horn Cairo quickly ducked back behind the boulder. It was cooler in the shadow of the great rock, and she leant back against it, closing her eyes against the momentary panic at the thought of facing Max. She could feel the cool, weatherworn stone pressing against her back. He was going to be very angry with her.

For a treacherous moment she contemplated staying hidden, before her pride reasserted itself and her spine stiffened. She wouldn't let herself be intimidated by Max Falconer, and, anyway, she didn't have any choice. If she stayed here, she had no way to get back to the safety of the camp.

Don't be such a coward, she reprimanded herself sternly and forced herself upright. What could he do to her, after all?

Taking a deep breath, Cairo walked out from behind the boulder. 'Hello.'

Max had his back to her and was bent over his rucksack, but at her greeting he spun round and stared incredulously at Cairo, slim and elegant in long, loose shorts and a sleeveless shirt. A large straw hat dangled from her hand.

'What the hell are you doing here?' he exploded, after a moment of stunned silence.

'Waiting for you,' she said, trying to sound composed.

There was a menacing pause. 'Do you have some problem understanding plain English?' asked Max with dangerous control. 'I've told you before, woman, and this is the last time I'm going to tell you, so you'd better listen hard.' He leant towards her, enunciating very slowly and clearly. 'I am not taking you up on to the plateau.'

Cairo quailed at the blaze of anger in his eyes, but held her ground. 'In that case, I'll just follow you,' she said bravely. 'You won't be able to do anything about it.'

'You'd never be able to keep up,' he said with dismissive contempt. 'You'd be lost within five minutes.'

'Perhaps, but you haven't left me with any other option,' Cairo said, her chin still tilted at a belligerent angle.

'Oh, yes, I have. Your only option is to take yourself back to the camp, and then to London, as soon as possible.'

'I can't.'

'What do you mean, you can't? You got here, didn't you? Now you can get yourself back.'

'I told the driver I was meeting you here. He's already left.'

There was a silence. 'Do you mean to tell me,' said Max, in a quiet voice that chilled Cairo to the bone, 'that you came out here to stand in a hundred and twenty degrees and sent away your one chance of survival?'

'I knew you would come,' said Cairo, forced back, despite herself, on to the defensive. 'Bruce said you usually came this way.'

'Usually, yes! But not always.' Max stared at her in disbelief. 'How could you be so stupidly irresponsible? I suppose you realise that if I had decided to go another way this morning you'd have been stranded? Nobody else comes here at this time of year, and you wouldn't stand a snowball's chance of walking back to the camp from here!'

'I have to get up on to the plateau,' Cairo said stubbornly.

'What is it with you?' Max's voice rose to a shout of sheer frustration. 'What's so important about this wretched advertisement that you have to risk your life for it?'

Cairo felt her cheeks burning, and set her jaw. 'I've just set up in partnership with a friend. It's taken ages to get our first job, and now that we've got it I can't go home and say that I couldn't even get myself to the location.' Her green eyes met his squarely. 'I don't want to climb up to this plateau any more than you want to take me, but I *have* to get there. If I don't, our business will fail. We won't get another chance like this.' There was no need to mention her godmother's loan weighing heavily on her shoulders, or her father, a broken man, waiting patiently for her to set him back on his feet.

'You were stupid to take on a job like this,' Max said unsympathetically. 'The desert's no place for a girl like you.'

Cairo lifted her chin proudly. 'You don't know what I'm like.'

'I can make a pretty good guess.' He looked at her with dislike. 'You've been pampered and indulged so much of your life that you think the world revolves around you, and you're prepared to ride roughshod over everyone just to get your own way. Never mind that I might not want to take you. Never mind that you might hold me up or distract me from my work. Never mind that if you were stuck here other people would risk their own lives, let alone their time and money, looking for you.' His jaw worked furiously. 'I ought to call your bluff and leave you here.'

Cairo held her breath as he turned away and swore, snatching off his hat and raking his fingers through his hair in frustration. 'You're a damned nuisance!' he ground out between his teeth. 'I can't afford the time to take you back to camp, and, as you've so cleverly calculated, I can hardly leave you to die of thirst, no matter how much you may deserve it.'

'So you'll take me with you?' Cairo beamed with relief, but her smile faded as Max stepped towards her and took her chin in one strong, brown hand.

He forced her face up so that her defiant green eyes were staring up into his, and she swallowed at the menacing expression that she read there. 'You may have won this round, but I wouldn't feel too smug about it if I were you, Cairo Kingswood,' he said. 'I don't take kindly to being manipulated, and if I hear one word of complaint, one *murmur* of protest about the conditions, I swear I'll abandon you right where you are.' His fingers were digging into her jaw, hurting her. 'Is that understood?'

'Yes,' she said. She wanted to sound cool and was humiliated to find that her voice came out as no more than a whisper.

'Good.' He released her, and she stepped back, instinctively rubbing her face where he had held her. The soft skin seemed to burn with the imprint of his fingers.

She would probably have two huge bruises tomorrow, Cairo thought resentfully.

'I presume you brought some supplies with you?' Max went on, impervious to her aggrieved looks. Having accepted the situation, however reluctantly, he was suddenly all brisk efficiency.

'I've got a backpack,' she said huskily.

'Show me.'

Cairo retrieved her rucksack and handed it over to Max, who emptied it out unceremoniously on to the ground. 'What are you doing?'

'The more you have to carry, the more you're going to slow me up. You won't need half of this stuff. This can go for a start.' He took her make-up bag and chucked it to one side.

'But that's got my cleanser and moisturiser in it!' she protested.

'If we find a guelta—an oasis—you can wash. Otherwise you'll just have to go dirty,' Max said curtly. 'There isn't much point in trying to impress me, and I'm the only person you'll be seeing.'

'I wouldn't bother to waste my time impressing *you*,' Cairo snapped back. 'I was thinking more in terms of personal hygiene.'

Max threw a towel over to join the make-up bag. 'And I'm thinking in terms of survival. You can do as I say on this trip, or you can stay behind. The choice is yours.'

Cairo subsided into muttering silence, watching sullenly as Max tossed out half the things she had carefully packed that morning. She had read a book about desert survival and had been rather pleased with herself for being so practical. When the compass went sailing through the air to join the pile, she was stung into protest.

'I might need that!'

'What for?'

'Well . . . something might happen to you.'

'You'd better hope that it doesn't,' Max said grimly. 'A compass isn't any use if you don't know where you're

going. You'd never find your way down alone, compass
or no compass.'

'I'm not leaving my Filofax.' Cairo pounced on it
before Max could chuck it on to the rapidly growing
pile, and clutched it protectively to her chest as if she
held her life in her hands, which was what it felt like.
She couldn't imagine functioning without it. It held ad-
dresses and phone numbers and bank account numbers
and notes about the business and lists and
birthdays... everything she ever needed to refer to had
been carefully entered into the black book and she wasn't
about to leave it behind, no matter what Max said.

'You won't need to make any appointments where
you're going,' Max pointed out sardonically. 'And there's
not much point in having someone's fax number when
you're dying of thirst.'

'I don't care. I'm not risking leaving it behind. I'd
feel lost without it.'

He shrugged. 'Suit yourself. But don't blame me when
you're struggling to carry your pack.' He ran a critical
eye over what was left in the dust; a torch, two large
water bottles, a bag of food, a sleeping sheet and mat
that a friend had lent her, an oversized T-shirt and spare
underwear. 'That's more than enough,' he grunted and
began repacking it all into her rucksack, while Cairo
surreptitiously retrieved her make-up bag.

When he came to her frivolous pants, he looked at
them, shaking his head as he stuffed them into the pack,
but contented himself with an ironic look.

Cairo flushed. 'What about my other things?' she
asked sharply.

'What about them?'

'I can't just leave them here. Someone might steal
them.'

'If I thought anyone would be along to steal them,
I'd leave you here for them to deal with,' said Max
bluntly. 'Leave them behind that boulder over there and
put a white stone on top of them. Then if anyone *did*

come along, they'd know it was someone else's property—always supposing they were interested in that rubbish. I can't imagine anyone finding a use for make-up in the desert.'

Cairo shifted her make-up bag to an unobtrusive position, and managed to slip it into her rucksack with the Filofax while Max was hunting for a white stone. She straightened quickly as he came back and met his suspicious look with an expression of limpid innocence.

'What are you doing?'

'Nothing. I await your next command.'

His brows drew together at her flippant tone. 'You don't seem to realise what a serious position you've put yourself in. You might have escaped being stranded, but you've still got to survive the next few days, and I don't think you're going to like it very much. Quite apart from anything else, you're completely dependent on me, so, if you don't want to find yourself in for a nasty shock, you'd be wise to tread *very carefully*,' he said with a note of unmistakable warning.

Cairo tossed back her hair defiantly. 'I'm not quite as helpless as you seem to think. I've got myself this far, haven't I?'

'You've got yourself into a very risky situation,' Max retorted. 'If you had any brains at all, you wouldn't be making flippant comments. You ought to be very nervous indeed about putting yourself in the hands of an entirely strange man, with no way of getting help.'

'I trust you,' said Cairo sullenly. She could see the truth of what Max was saying, but she hated looking foolish, and, although she disliked him intensely, for some reason it had never occurred to her to distrust him.

'More fool you,' said Max. 'I might be a sex-starved madman for all you know.'

She had got the point the first time, Cairo thought crossly. 'You don't seem to be mad,' she said in a cold voice. 'Rude and unpleasant, yes. Mad, no. As for sex-starved, well, it's perfectly obvious that you don't like women.'

Max's eyes narrowed. 'What makes you so sure about that?' He moved towards her, and, suddenly nervous, Cairo backed away until she came up against the big boulder. Her heart was thumping against her ribs, but she met his eyes defiantly.

'You've gone out of your way to give me that impression!'

He was standing very close. 'You're so sure of yourself, aren't you?' he said softly. 'Just because I haven't shown any interest in you, you automatically assume that I couldn't possibly be interested in anyone else.' Taking her wrists, he pinned them against the boulder. The look on his face made Cairo struggle to free herself, but his grip was like steel. 'What's it like to be that vain?' he asked conversationally.

Cairo had no chance to answer, for the next moment he had bent his head to kiss her. She tried desperately to turn her face away, but he anticipated her, capturing her mouth with his own. The touch of his lips sent a shock of electric awareness surging through her, and she gave an involuntary gasp which opened her lips to his demand. His mouth was hard, insistent as it explored hers, and, horrified at her instinctive leap of response, Cairo fought to contain the excitement uncurling treacherously along her senses.

Max shifted position slightly, letting his body press her back against the rock while he dropped her wrists to tangle his fingers in her thick golden hair. The vast desert landscape had spun and shrunk around Cairo, until there was nothing except the massive solidity of the boulder behind her, and Max, his mouth on hers and his hands against her face, and the taut, tantalising power of his body. Her hands had fallen limply when he released them, but as his kisses deepened they crept instinctively up his arms, her fingers tightening against the

rough khaki cotton of his shirt as if uncertain whether
to pull him closer or push him away.

Cairo felt as if the ground had dropped from beneath
her feet. Her body seemed to have acquired a will of its
own, relaxing against Max; ignoring her frantic attempts to keep control, her lips had abandoned themselves to the thrilling pressure of his mouth, and her eyes
had closed as they gave themselves up to the dangerous,
shocking, shaming pleasure of his touch.

With a muttered exclamation, Max drew away abruptly, and Cairo sagged back against the boulder,
grateful for its support. Her legs felt weak and her eyes
were huge and dazed by the sudden return to reality.

A muscle was beating furiously in Max's jaw, and his
eyes were blazing with an emotion Cairo couldn't
identify, but otherwise he had himself well under control.
He wasn't even breathing hard. As she remembered how
she had melted into his kiss, a tide of colour swept up
Cairo's throat and stained her cheeks crimson. She
spread her hands against the boulder and pushed herself
upright rather shakily.

'That wasn't fair,' she whispered.

'You asked for it,' said Max in a hard voice. 'As it
happens, I do like women, but only some, and your
brand of rather unsubtle charm leaves me stone cold.'

'Why kiss me, then?'

'To teach you a lesson. You've put yourself entirely
in my power, and you've no one to blame but yourself.'
Max looked at her with a contempt that deepened the
colour in her cheeks. 'I don't like you and I don't want
you with me, so don't ask me to be *fair* with you, Cairo.
You haven't earned the right.'

Swinging up his rucksack, he shrugged it on to his
back. 'As far as I'm concerned, you can stay here and
die of thirst,' he said, as he fastened the buckle at his
waist and adjusted the straps. 'But if you're coming,
you'd better get a move-on. I'm not wasting any more

of my time.' Without waiting to see whether she had moved or not, he turned away and set off up the path.

Cairo stared after him with loathing. Her heart was still pounding from his kiss, and she was struggling to bring her breathing under control. At that moment, dying of thirst seemed infinitely preferable to ever seeing Max Falconer again. She would have given anything she possessed to have walked away in the opposite direction, but as her humiliation cooled reason returned. As Max had pointed out, she hadn't left herself with any choice.

He was walking steadily upwards, his brown skin and dull clothes blending into the stony background. He hadn't looked back once. Cairo bit her lip and pulled herself together with an effort. She wouldn't put it past him to leave her behind. Hoisting her pack on to her back, and jamming her hat on to her head, she set out after him.

The first bit of the path leading up to the very edge of the plateau was steep and narrow, and every now and then her trainers would slip, skidding rubble in all directions. It was oppressively hot and the sun bounced off the rock, enveloping her in its harsh glare. Cairo's breath was soon coming in short gasps. Beneath her hat, her hair was damp with sweat and clung uncomfortably to her neck.

Ahead of her, Max walked with a loose, rhythmic stride. He looked cool and comfortable, and his indifference grated on Cairo's resentful nerves. He hadn't so much as glanced to see whether she was following or not! He was obviously hoping that she wouldn't be able to keep up, and Cairo was equally determined to prove him wrong. Gritting her teeth, she toiled upwards.

Hating Max made it easier to ignore the hot air which dried in her lungs, making it hard to breathe, or the way the straps of the backpack rubbed against her shoulders. She had never met anyone who made so little effort to hide his dislike. He had every right to be angry at the way she had forced herself upon him, but there had been no need to assault her like that!

Cairo's hot face grew even hotter as she remembered how humiliatingly she had responded to his touch. It was only because he had taken her by surprise, she argued to herself. Max Falconer was the very last type of man she would find attractive. That cold, hard look had never appealed to her, and, if his mouth had been unexpectedly warm and exciting, well, that was just part of the sudden shock of being kissed like that. She wished she couldn't remember how it had felt quite so vividly. Her senses still quivered, and her stomach churned at the thought of the hard strength of her body. He *wasn't* attractive. He was just...unexpected.

Cairo paused for breath and wiped the sweat off her upper lip as she looked around her. The path was twisting its way up a narrow gorge, and the rock walls soared above her, trapping the heat so that it pressed down on her like a leaden weight. It was a terrible place, she thought with a shudder, bare and menacing. She longed for the soft greenness of England, for a glimpse of trees and fields and houses. Even the immense emptiness of the desert below them would be preferable to this!

Trudging on with her head bent, it was some time before she noticed that Max had stopped above her and was waiting in the shade of an overhanging rock. The thought of a rest quickened her step. She would expire from heat and thirst if she didn't sit down for a while.

Max sat on the stony ground, arms resting on his knees, and head turned to watch her plod the last few yards uphill towards him. Cairo was very conscious of her red face and the sweat trickling down her back, and she was bitterly resentful of the cool amusement she could detect lurking around his mouth. She knew he was comparing the elegant woman who had approached him yesterday afternoon with the hot, dishevelled girl who was puffing and panting towards him now. She scowled at him as she unbuckled her rucksack and pulled out her water.

'You'll have to make better time than this if you want to make it to the camp site before dark,' said Max.

'I'm going as fast as I can,' Cairo snapped, intent on unscrewing her water bottle. The water was warm and brackish, but she tipped back her head and let it splash over her face and pour down her parched throat as if it were nectar. Satisfied at last, she took off her hat, pushed her sunglasses on top of her head and wiped her wet face with the back of her hand.

Max got to his feet as she screwed the top back on and put the bottle back in her rucksack. 'Ready?'

Cairo opened her mouth to protest that she hadn't had time to rest when she met his eyes. He was just waiting for her to complain! Well, let him wait! She wasn't giving in that easily. She lifted her chin at him, green eyes bright with challenge, and swung her pack back on her back. 'Ready,' she said, and pushed the straw hat back into place.

There was a flash of reluctant admiration in Max's eyes before he turned away. Cairo felt insensibly cheered as she settled her glasses back on her nose and took a deep breath. She would show him! Her legs felt shaky, and she longed to collapse in a heap in the shade, but the thought of Max's contempt forced her to put one foot in front of the other, and she trudged doggedly after him.

If she hadn't known better, she would have thought that it was for her sake that Max stopped again, not too long afterwards. He shrugged off his pack in the deep shade of a crevice as Cairo climbed slowly up towards him.

'We'll rest here for a while.'

She dropped down beside him and closed her eyes, too tired to even find her water bottle. Her heart was pounding with effort and her head felt as if it was held in a vice of heat and glare and thirst.

'Here,' said Max gruffly, and she opened her eyes to see him holding out an orange which he had cut into quarters with his knife. They were green on the outside, but juicy and orange within, and Cairo sucked at them greedily. She had never tasted anything as delicious before.

'Thank you,' she mumbled through the pith. The sweetness had an immediate effect, and when she had found herself a drink and wiped her face, she felt much better. Taking off her hat and glasses, she ran her fingers through her damp hair and lay back against her pack again with a sigh.

'Why are you doing this?' asked Max abruptly. 'All this talk about doing your job just doesn't ring true somehow. You don't strike me as a career type.'

He was right there, thought Cairo. Until a year ago, she had never had to work at all, but that was a year ago. Things had changed since then.

'I'm doing it for the same reason most people do their jobs,' she said. 'I need the money.'

'There must be easier ways of making money than putting yourself through this.' Max glanced over at Cairo, slumped against her pack, her golden hair dark with sweat and her long legs sprawled out in front of her in the dust. Her trainers and short white socks had been pristine white that morning; now they were brown and ingrained with sand. 'This consultancy business sounds like a lot of hot air. Why don't you get yourself a proper job?'

Cairo fanned herself with her hat. 'I haven't got any qualifications,' she admitted. There had been no need for her to get a job after she had left school, and she had drifted on, always talking about doing some course, but never getting around to it until it was too late.

'It's hard to believe it from the way you've carried on since you've been here, but I presume you've got a brain somewhere in your head,' said Max caustically. 'There must be something you can do.'

That was what *she* had thought, thought Cairo, remembering bitterly the long months when she had tried to get a job, any job; those humiliating agency interviews when she had to admit that she had no qualifications and no experience, the endless letters of rejection, the slow, painful realisation that as far as the world was concerned she was completely useless. Her confidence had been gradually eroded, so that in the end she had been delighted to get work as a waitress. That was before she'd run into Piers again. He was the one who'd picked her up and restored her confidence and made her realise that she had been on quite the wrong track.

'You can get by on ordinary jobs,' she said to Max. 'But if you want to make big money, you've got to take a risk. If our consultancy is a success, we'll make far more money than if we'd stuck at a nice, safe job.'

'Oh, *money*!' sneered Max. 'I might have known that it would come down to that. Is that all that's important to you?'

Cairo thought of her father's face as he added up his debts. 'It is at the moment,' she said evenly. Suddenly, she wanted to cry and make Max understand, but he had obviously given up in disgust, stretching out in the shade and tipping his hat over his eyes.

It was the first time she had been able to look at him properly. He was wearing shabby trousers and an old khaki shirt, its long sleeves carelessly rolled up above his wrists, and open to reveal the strong brown column of his neck. She found her eyes drawn to the pulse beating slow and steady at the base of his throat. His hands were linked behind his head and he looked utterly relaxed and at home in this stark, alien environment.

She glanced around her. The rocks seemed to press in on every side, the walls of the chasm looming above her, and the path twisting up and up above them, littered with rock falls. The silence hung hot and heavy. Far, far above her, in the narrow strip of sky, an eagle hung apparently motionless on a thermal current.

Cairo shivered. How could Max look so . . . so *right* in this awful place? She shifted imperceptibly closer, remembering what he had said about her utter dependence on him. His solid strength was overwhelmingly reassuring, and her fingers tingled with the unnerving realisation that she wanted to reach out and touch him.

Cairo remembered wryly how disappointed she had been when she had first seen him. She had been distinctly unimpressed, but one look in his eyes had been enough to realise that Max was no more the quiet, ordinary man he had appeared from a distance than he was the flamboyantly romantic figure of her imagination. There was an intriguingly detached quality about him, an air of self-sufficiency, as if he had not the slightest interest in anyone else or what they might think of him. Cairo doubted if he had.

Her gaze lingered on him speculatively. He would be easier to deal with if he were as cold as he appeared at first sight, she thought, but his eyes revealed a man much more passionate beneath the surface. It left Cairo with a feeling of potentially explosive tension which was as unsettling as it was elusively familiar. She had sensed it before, she knew she had.

Her eyes strayed to his mouth, the only part of his face not covered by his hat. Just looking at it gave her a strange feeling, and her lips seemed to burn once more with the memory of his kisses. No, he wasn't nearly as cold as he liked to appear.

Unaware of her scrutiny, Max wriggled his shoulders into a more comfortable position, and Cairo drew a sharp breath, startled by a sharp jab of sudden, unaccountable, unwanted desire.

'What's the matter?' Max lifted his hat at her indrawn gasp and squinted at her. Even in the shadow, his light eyes were uncomfortably penetrating, and Cairo looked quickly away.

'Nothing,' she said in a strangled voice. Horrified at her own reaction, she cleared her throat and improvised hastily, 'That is, I was just wondering if we might have met before.'

Max gave a hard look and then, much to her relief, dropped his hat back over his eyes. 'I hardly think we move in the same circles, do you?' he said dismissively.

'No.' He was irritating, overbearing, arrogant, intolerant and downright rude, Cairo reminded herself fiercely, unable to stop her eyes sliding back up his throat to that unexpectedly sensual mouth. The heat must have affected her more than she had thought. She searched around for something to say, desperate to keep on talking and keep her mind off Max's mouth and Max's body and the way Max's fingers had tangled in her hair.

'What do you do, exactly?'

'I'm a geologist.' Max sounded resigned at her question. 'I'm doing a survey of the structures and potential minerals of the plateau for the Shofrar government at the moment.'

'Do you work for the same company as Bruce Mitchell?'

'No, I'm an independent consultant.'

'A consultant?' Cairo was unable to prevent mimicking his comment to her. 'Why don't you get a proper job?'

'I work best on my own,' said Max, unperturbed, but a reluctant smile bracketed his mouth, sending a disquieting jolt of warmth through Cairo.

She jerked her eyes away. 'Have you been working here long?'

'What is this? A cocktail party?' He tilted his hat to send her a sardonic look. 'This kind of interrogation reminds me of London parties. Everyone interrogates you in the same way—"What do you do? Do you enjoy it?"—and all the time their eyes are sliding over your shoulder, looking for someone more interesting to talk to. It's all gush and superficial charm. Why do you bother if you're not interested?'

'I *am* interested,' said Cairo, wondering about the bitterness that edged his voice when he talked about London. 'I wouldn't bother wasting any charm on you, superficial or otherwise, but, for better or worse, we are travelling together,' she added reasonably. 'I just thought it would be nice to know a little more about you. If I hadn't really wanted to know how long you'd been here, I wouldn't have asked.'

Max sighed. 'If it's that fascinating, the answer's about seven years.'

'Don't you ever want to go home?'

'What to?' He pushed back his hat and sat up, resting his back against the rock. 'I grew up in a city, and I never want to go back there. It's all nice and civilised on the surface, but underneath it's rotten to the core. Most of the people I knew were obsessed with money— just like you—and if it wasn't money, it was with protecting appearances at all costs, with pretending to be what they weren't. Corruption starts at that level, and I found it nauseating.'

Cairo winced. Her father had been vilified in the Press for being corrupt, and the label still stung. Corrupt suggested someone devious and rotten, as Max had said, but her father had never been that. Foolhardy, perhaps, even dishonest, but not *bad*. How could she explain to Max that someone who had broken the law in his business dealings could also be kind and loyal and absurdly generous?

'Things aren't always as black and white as you make out,' she said after a moment.

'No,' he agreed unexpectedly. 'They're not. But they are in the desert. That's why I like it here.' His eyes were on the eagle, circling effortlessly high above them. 'The desert strips a man down to the essentials. Time takes on a different meaning out here. There are no images in the desert, no worrying about making an impression. You are what you are.' He glanced at Cairo suddenly, his eyes light and sharp. 'You ought to spend more time in the desert. It might make you less tense.'

'I am not tense!' said Cairo, nettled, and turned her face away deliberately, determined not to show any more interest.

CHAPTER THREE

THEY sat on in silence. Max had an ability to sit absolutely still, Cairo noticed, watching him huffily out of the corner of her eye. His eyes were shadowed by his hat, and it was impossible to tell what he was thinking.

He baffled and intrigued Cairo. He was so unlike any man she had met before, and, much as she wanted to ignore him, she couldn't help speculating what had brought him to the desert in the first place. Something must have caused that burning hostility to city life. Was it a woman? Had his heart been broken by a girl who loved money more than she loved him? He didn't *look* like the kind of man who would break his heart over a woman. He was too self-sufficient for that.

Cairo slid another glance over towards him, wondering what sort of girl Max would love. She wouldn't be tall or blonde or sophisticated, that was for sure, she thought with a pang of something that was almost like jealousy. She had never met anyone so unresponsive to her charms.

Tracing patterns in the dust with her finger, Cairo realised that she didn't like imagining Max with another woman, smiling at her, touching her, running his hard hands over her skin... She felt her spine shiver at the thought, and she glanced at him again, only to find him watching her with an unreadable expression.

Their eyes met with a jarring contact, and the tension seemed to jump suddenly between them. Cairo found herself flushing, certain that he knew she was remembering how he had kissed her.

'We'd better go,' said Max abruptly.

'Yes.' Cairo scrambled to her feet, too glad of the diversion to remember how tired she felt, but she grimaced as she heaved the rucksack back on to her shoulders. It seemed to have doubled in weight, and rubbed uncomfortably against her skin.

'It looks like you've got a bit of sunburn there.' Max's finger brushed inadvertently against her shoulder as he pointed, and she flinched as if from an electric shock. He raised a sardonic eyebrow. 'I thought you weren't tense?'

'I'm not,' she said between clenched teeth. 'It's just a bit sore.'

Max was typically unsympathetic. 'Serves you right for wearing a sleeveless shirt. This is no time to be getting a tan.'

'Actually, I was thinking of staying cool,' said Cairo crossly.

'You'll stay much cooler with a thin layer on.' Max gave an irritable sigh and opened his rucksack. After digging around for a moment, he pulled out a faded shirt in a dull, muddy green colour. 'Here,' he said, tossing it over to her. 'Put that on. I don't want you on my hands with sunstroke.'

His expression warned her not to argue. Wrinkling her nose at the colour, Cairo slipped it on over her sleeveless top. She couldn't get any hotter than she was, and anyway it would be worth it to stop the straps rubbing her shoulders. The shirt was far too big for her, so she rolled up the sleeves and knotted the tails loosely over her hips with an instinctive sense of style.

'Very *haute couture*,' said Max maliciously.

'Sludge-green is in this year,' she retorted with mock pretension, and the fact that Max almost smiled was enough to make her hardly notice her back as she heaved it on again.

Cairo lost track of time as the path wound its way up the gorge in an endless series of hairpin bends. At times, she found herself edging along the rock wall, with a vertiginous drop down to the bottom of the gorge at the other side of the narrow path, and, although she didn't suffer from vertigo, she was glad that Max waited for her at those parts.

Her face was white and tense after the first of these ordeals, and Max frowned as he saw her wipe her face with a trembling hand.

'Are you all right?' he asked brusquely, and immediately Cairo's head came up.

'I'm fine.'

Still, she was immensely relieved when they finally made it to the top of the gorge, hours later. 'You've done the worst bit,' said Max. 'It's relatively flat from now on.'

Cairo was breathing too hard to reply, or even wonder at his encouragement, but she nodded her head gratefully as she reached for her water bottle. Her fingers felt as if they had swollen to the size of sausages in the heat and she fumbled with the fastenings on her pack until Max opened it for her and unscrewed the water bottle with an exasperated shake of his head.

'Thank you,' she gasped, tipping it back, too thankful to resent his irritation.

When she lowered the bottle, she saw to her astonishment that Max was smiling and holding up a hand in greeting. Blinking, she looked over her shoulder to see two men loping towards them through the rocks, and for a moment she wondered if she were hallucinating. They wore plastic sandals and each had a string bag hung over his shoulder. They might have been popping down to the shops for a pint of milk.

'What are they doing here?' she whispered to Max as they came up, grinning.

'They're smugglers,' he said out of the corner of his mouth. 'Libya is just at the other side of the plateau. They bring in tea and take back chewing gum.' He squatted down with the two men and chatted as they smoked the cigarettes he offered them. Clearly excluded as a woman, Cairo sat awkwardly to one side. Max had an astonishingly attractive smile when he chose to use it, she noticed grudgingly. He never smiled like that at *her*. What was so special about the smugglers?

The two men had been giving her curious looks, and as they made to leave they smiled at her and called out some comment to Max. His reply made them laugh, and they dropped over the lip of the gorge on to the path with a cheery wave.

'What was all that about?' asked Cairo suspiciously.

'They think you're very beautiful.' Max's tone made it clear that he didn't share their opinion. 'They were just envying me my woman.'

'I hope you made it clear that I was no such thing,' Cairo said, piqued.

'Of course I didn't,' he said with an irritable look. 'Do you really want it known that a single, unprotected girl is wandering around the plateau up for grabs? Those men wouldn't be averse to smuggling a blonde girl into the country. You'd probably be worth a good deal more than a bag of chewing gum.'

'Nice of you to admit it!' said Cairo in a voice that dripped acid. 'I'm surprised you didn't offer me in exchange for their tea while you had the chance!'

'It would have been a bargain,' he retorted nastily. 'I wish I'd thought of it. A bag of tea would be lighter, easier and a lot more useful to take along with me than a spoilt blonde!'

Walking across the top of the plateau proved to be nearly as hard as climbing the gorge. It was flatter, but there was no path, and the ground varied from ankle-wrenching stones to flat, fissured rock and scattered boulders.

The sun was setting in a blaze of gold as Cairo trudged up a sloping seam of rock to where Max seemed to be standing at the edge of the world. His distinctive silhouette was sharply etched against the glowing sky, and in spite of her exhaustion she caught her breath at the sight.

When she reached him, she realised that they were standing on the edge of a wadi. Max pointed across it. 'See that tree over there? That's the camp.'

Cairo stared, speechless at the sight of the huge cedar, apparently growing out of nothing. After the unrelieved brown of the rocks she had been walking through all day, its green leaves seemed incredible. The fiery evening light suffused the air, softening the rocky landscape and touching the tree with gold.

'What a magical place,' she breathed.

Max glanced down at her. 'They say that tree is over three thousand years old.'

'But how can it live that long? There's no water, nothing.' For once Cairo forgot to be snappy with him.

'The desert used to be a much cooler, wetter place than it is now. When this tree was growing there was much more water around, and its roots are so deep now that when it does rain it can make the most of it.'

Cairo was silent as they climbed down into the wadi and up the other side, thinking of how much the world had changed since the tree had first started to grow. Now that the end was in sight, her exhaustion threatened to overwhelm her, and the last yards seemed to take forever. This time, though, Max walked beside her, and when she stumbled and would have fallen he caught her arm in a hard grasp and held her upright. The jolt of feeling at his touch revived Cairo, and she stiffened her legs so that she could walk up to the tree on her own.

Max let her collapse under the leaves, too tired to do anything but stare blankly up at the swollen water bag which hung from one of the branches. Made from an entire goatskin, it was hung up by its legs and dripped slowly on to the dusty ground.

'This is the camp used by tourists,' he said, nodding at some ragged canvas tents. 'Normally you have to stay in one of three designated areas, but as I'm working for the government I can camp wherever I need to.' He shot

Cairo an amused look. 'Make the most of your last taste of civilisation.'

Cairo looked up at the skin and then at the tatty tents. Civilisation? She gave a weak laugh. 'What have I done to deserve all this luxury tonight?'

'I've arranged for my supplies to be brought up by mule,' said Max, unruffled by her irony. Much to her annoyance, he was looking as cool and fresh as he had nearly twelve hours earlier. 'It means I can come back here and stock up with food and water when I need to, instead of carrying it all up the gorge with me. They come a much longer route, so they're not here yet. We'll have some tea with the caretaker while we wait.' He walked off towards the tents, ordering her over his shoulder to stay there, as if she were a dog.

She wouldn't have any trouble obeying that command, Cairo reflected wearily. She was so stiff and sore and tired that she couldn't have moved even if she had wanted to.

A few minutes later, Max reappeared with a grave, wizened old man who greeted Cairo serenely and calmly set about making them tea while Max talked to him. Cairo found his unhurried movements strangely soothing. Sitting crosslegged by the fire, he brewed some tea and mint with a pinch of sugar in a blue enamel teapot. When it had boiled, he poured the tea back and forth between the pot and a small glass. His fingers were deft as he flipped the lid of the teapot to pour in the tea from the glass and then held the pot high to let a long stream froth into the glass again. At length he was satisfied, and handed them a glass each.

Cairo sipped at the tea curiously. It was deliciously minty and reviving.

'You must drink three glasses, and three only,' said Max. 'The first is said to be bitter, like life. The second is strong like love, and the third is sweet like death.'

His deep voice seemed to quiver against Cairo's skin. She was very aware of him. He sat crosslegged like the old man, his knee only inches from hers, with his back to the sun so that the slanting light glowed around him. His head was bent courteously towards the caretaker, and she was struck once again at how different he was with other people. How could the man who bandied jokes with smugglers or talked quietly with an old man be the same man who looked at her with such hostility, or kissed her with such savage passion?

It was completely dark by the time a jingle of harness and the sliding sound of hoofs on rocks announced the arrival of Max's supplies. Cairo was beyond feeling hungry by then, but Max made her eat some of the couscous he heated up on his stove.

'It's all right,' she said when he offered her a tin bowl of the steaming stew. 'I've got my own food.'

'Don't be ridiculous, woman,' said Max irritably. 'You've got to eat something.'

'I'll have a biscuit.' She tugged the battered packet out of her rucksack. They looked stale and dry and unappetising.

'A few biscuit crumbs aren't going to get you very far.'

'I'm not that hungry. I'm too tired to eat much anyway.'

Max banged a spoon into the bowl and shoved it into her hands. 'I don't care how tired or hungry you are. You're going to eat,' he said forcefully. 'If you don't eat properly, you won't be able to walk, and I don't want to deal with you fainting with hunger halfway across the plateau.' He paused. 'Of course, it's just occurred to me that I could leave you here and send you down with the mules . . .'

'No! I'll have some.' Having got this far, Cairo was damned if she was going to allow herself to be sent back down without completing her job. She inspected the contents of the bowl dubiously, but when she tried it she found that it was deliciously spicy, and realised that she was ravenous after all. She cleaned the bowl and handed it back to Max rather guiltily. As there was only one bowl, he had to wait until she had finished before he could have his own meal. 'Thank you,' she said humbly.

Afterwards, Max made coffee and they shared the enamel mug, passing it wordlessly between them. Every time Cairo's fingers brushed against Max's on the handle, something within her would tighten dangerously. Nobody had ever had this effect on her before, especially not someone she disliked so intensely, and it made her feel edgy. Cairo put it down to exhaustion and the alien surroundings. It was very dark, and only the distant murmur of voices from the men by the mules reminded her that she and Max were not the only people in the world.

Max seemed quite unperturbed by her presence. He sat resting his arms on his knees, his hands loosely clasped together, gazing thoughtfully out into the darkness. Cairo watched him covertly. It was that quality of self-containment that was so naggingly familiar, she decided. Perhaps not precisely *familiar*, she amended to herself, but somehow recognisable. This lurking sense that she had met him before was beginning to annoy her. It had happened too many times for it to be explained by a mere trick of the mind. Somehow, somewhere, she had come across Max—or someone who was very like him.

'Have you got any family?' she asked him, breaking the silence.

Max turned his head to look at her. She half expected him to be as brusque as when she had asked him about his work, but he said only, 'A sister. Why?'

'It's just that I keep getting this weird feeling that I know you. I wondered if you had a brother I might have met somewhere.'

'No, there's just me and Joanna.'

'Joanna's your sister? Maybe I've met *her*.' Sometimes brothers and sisters could look quite different and yet share certain family characteristics. 'Is she like you?'

In the flickering firelight, Max looked almost amused. 'No. If anything, she's more like *you*.'

'Me?' Cairo echoed in astonishment.

'Oh, she doesn't look anything like you. Joanna's pretty in a quiet sort of way, but she certainly doesn't have your flamboyant style. She doesn't have your confidence either, but you're alike in other respects. You're both city girls, for a start. She can't understand why I choose to live in the desert any more than you seem to. Joanna's idea of the outdoor life is sitting on a terrace, with perhaps the occasional trek all the way across the pavement to the car.'

'I'm not like that!' Cairo said indignantly.

'Aren't you? I can't see you going out for a bracing walk in the country when you could be in some over-heated shop or restaurant.'

'Well . . .' Cairo tried to remember the last time she had even been to the country, let alone for a walk. 'I don't need to go for a walk,' she said at last. 'I take plenty of exercise. I go to the gym every day at home,' she added proudly.

'Still safely inside,' he mocked. 'I don't know why girls like you and Joanna are so afraid of fresh air. You seem content to live in a completely artificial environment.'

'Rubbish!'

'It's not rubbish. You expect electricity at a flick of a switch, water at the turn of a tap, you go everywhere in cars, individual metal boxes that seal you off from the rest of the world. It doesn't really matter to you what the weather is like. All you care about is what you're going to wear. Will it be the silk dress or something you can wear with a jacket?' He mimicked an agony of indecision, and Cairo gave an uncomfortable laugh. He reminded her all too clearly of the days when she had had nothing to do but wonder what to wear.

'Are you like this with Joanna?'

'Like what?'

'You seem very critical of her lifestyle—not to mention mine. I hope she tells you what you can do with your opinions!'

Max gave rather a twisted grin. 'That wouldn't be Joanna's style. She wouldn't dare, and I suppose, because I know that, I don't criticise her.'

'You don't seem to have had any of those inhibitions with me,' Cairo pointed out tartly.

'You're more than capable of standing up for yourself,' he said with a hint of amusement. 'I haven't noticed you not daring to answer back.'

'I don't suppose anyone ever answers you back,' Cairo grumbled. 'In fact, there probably isn't anyone *to* answer you back out here. No wonder you don't like anyone disagreeing with you. You're far too used to having your own way.'

'Funny, I would have said exactly the same thing about you,' said Max, a touch acidly. 'You've been pampered and indulged all your life. You're like some hothouse plant that can't survive out of its carefully controlled environment. A breath of cold air, a nasty brush with the real world, and you're lost. You don't stand a chance in a harsh environment like the desert.'

'Perhaps,' said Cairo. 'But here I am.' She tilted her chin and her defiant eyes met his across the fire.

'Yes,' Max said slowly, as if the idea was new to him. 'Here you are.'

There was an uneasy pause. Cairo dropped her gaze, unable to look at him any longer. She felt as if she had stepped on to suddenly shaky ground without being sure why.

'Er—where do I sleep?' she asked awkwardly. Anything to break the silence. 'In the tents?'

'If you want, but I suggest you sleep with me,' said Max, and Cairo's nerves jerked at the image his words conjured up.

'With you?' she squeaked, and Max lifted an eyebrow.

'There's no need to carry on like an outraged spinster. I wasn't about to suggest a night of unbridled passion,' he said drily. 'You're already an object of much speculation among the men, and I'd advise you not to spoil the impression that you're my woman by going off alone, that's all.'

Cairo bit her lip. She found the thought of sleeping near him infinitely disturbing, but she could see that his suggestion was a sensible one. 'Where are you sleeping, if not in the tents?' she asked at last, trying to sound reasonable.

'Right here.' Max untied a sleeping mat from the top of his rucksack and tossed it down by the fire.

'What, on the ground?'

'Yes, on the ground,' he confirmed with exaggerated patience. 'What were you expecting? A five-star motel?'

'I don't know...I hadn't thought...' Cairo stood irresolute. 'A tent, perhaps?' She glanced over her shoulder to where she could just make out the shape of the tents behind the tree. 'Why don't we sleep over there?'

'Because I like to sleep under the stars. I don't like a roof over my head, it makes me feel trapped.'

Cairo looked at him curiously. Trapped? It was a revealing choice of word. 'You must have to sleep under a roof sometimes. How do you manage when you're in England?'

'I'm not neurotic about it.' Max shrugged. 'But given the choice, I'd rather sleep outside than in.'

'That's all very well when you're on your own, but what about when you're with other people?'

'Like you?'

'No, I meant...someone closer. A wife, for instance,' she suggested.

Max glanced at her as he unrolled his sleeping bag. 'I'm not married.'

'But if you were?' Cairo persisted. 'Would you drag a wife up here and make her sleep under the stars?'

'Most of the time there isn't anywhere else to sleep,' he pointed out. 'You seem very concerned, Cairo. What does it matter to you what my wife—admittedly a very unlikely eventuality—would have to put up with?'

Cairo could feel herself flushing, and was glad of the darkness. 'It doesn't matter,' she said, studying her hands. 'I was just curious about whether you imagined yourself spending your whole life alone out here. Don't you miss your family and friends?'

'My friends are here,' said Max. 'And as for family...well, there's Joanna, of course, but she leads such a different life. I just don't fit in there any more. I don't think I ever did.' He stared into the flames. 'Sometimes I imagine myself living in a nice house like hers, going into work every day, sitting in some office week after week, and I come out in a cold sweat at the very thought. So yes, I suppose I do see myself staying out here—or somewhere like here.'

'Don't you ever get lonely?' she asked.

He seemed to have forgotten she was there, but at her question, he looked across at her with a sardonic expression. 'What a feminine question! Don't you mean, why don't I get married?'

'Well, why don't you?'

'Because the only females I ever seem to come across are more at home in nightclubs than lying under the stars,' Max said flatly. 'If I marry anyone, it'll be a girl who can cope with the desert, who loves it as much as I do, not one who's forever pining for the comforts of home.'

His eyes rested on Cairo disparagingly, and she ruffled up, certain that he was thinking that she was exactly the type of girl he would least like to marry. Well, he needn't think it bothered her! She didn't have the slightest desire to spend her life in a place like this. Max could sneer all he wanted at his sister's house, but Cairo would have given anything to have been there now. It would be clean and warm. There would be electric light, and a bed with a mattress and sheets. All they had here was the flickering light of the fire and a sleeping mat to lay upon the stony ground.

'You'd better get some sleep,' said Max abruptly, as if regretting having said as much as he had. 'You've a long walk in the morning.'

'Can't I wash first?' Cairo asked, glad of the change of subject.

'You can if you're prepared to make do with a wet cloth. There's no bathroom *en suite*, as you can see.'

Cairo was grimy with dust and sweat, and there was nothing she wanted more at that moment than to be safely at home in her clean blue and white bathroom with its deep bath and soft towels and comforting clutter of jars and bottles on the shelf below the mirror, but she took the flannel Max handed her with only a tiny sigh.

'Where shall I go?' she asked, looking round her.

'What's wrong with here?'

'I'd prefer to take my clothes off in private,' she said coldly.

'I'm sure you would, but if you wander around in the dark with no clothes on, you're likely to tread on a scorpion.'

'A s-scorpion?' Cairo echoed uncertainly. 'Are there really scorpions around here?'

Max gave a grim smile. 'And snakes. And spiders. And, like most creatures of the desert, they come out at night, so I'd be careful where I was treading if I were you.'

Cairo glanced nervously about her, half expecting to see swarms of creepy-crawlies lurking at the edge of the firelight. Suddenly the darkness didn't seem quite so invitingly private.

'Look, stop dithering around,' sighed Max at last. 'If you're going to wash, wash—but don't use too much water.' He thrust a container of water towards her, adding sardonically, 'I'll be a gentleman and promise not to

look, but for God's sake get on with it. You're not the
only one who wants to get to bed.'

He turned his back ostentatiously to face the fire, and
Cairo seized the opportunity to pull her make-up bag
out of her rucksack. She was glad she had brought it
along now! At least she was able to clean her face
properly. She retreated to the shadows, very conscious
of Max's proximity, but was so desperate to wash that
she stripped off her clothes and did the best she could
with the flannel.

'Haven't you finished yet?' demanded Max as she was
rubbing moisturiser into her legs.

'Don't look round!'

'I'm not going to look round,' he said, exasperated.
'I just wondered what you'd found to do with that flannel
that could possibly take you that long. It's obviously far
more versatile than I ever gave it credit for!'

'I like to feel clean,' Cairo explained, wriggling into
a T-shirt. It was long and loose and fell halfway down
her thighs, and she was glad Max had left her something
clean and comfortable to sleep in.

She could practically hear him rolling his eyes. 'I don't
know why you're bothering. You're only going to get
dirty again tomorrow.'

Cairo ignored him. His perfect woman might not care
whether she washed or not, but she wasn't in the running
for *that* role anyway, and it would take a lot more than
Max Falconer's disapproval to interrupt her beauty
routine.

Unrolling her sleeping mat, she laid it out near
Max's—but not too near—with a show of unconcern.
She would take his advice about not sleeping on her own,
but she didn't want to get too close. She had had enough
of Max Falconer for one day!

'Decided you prefer me to the scorpions?' He had
glanced over his shoulder, and for a moment his expression was arrested as he caught sight of Cairo bending
over her rucksack. Her legs were long and slender be-

neath her T-shirt, and her hair caught the firelight as it fell forward to hide her face.

'Marginally,' she said coldly, without looking at him.

He watched her as she shook out her sleeping sheet and laid it on the mat. It looked flimsy and very close to the ground, she thought nervously. There wouldn't be much between her and a scorpion, not to mention the snakes and the spiders.

'Why on earth didn't you bring a sleeping bag?' asked Max sharply, almost as if he could read her mind.

'I didn't think I'd need one. This is the Sahara, after all.'

'And in all the famous research you supposedly did before you came, did you never come across the information that the Sahara gets very cold at night?'

'I can't believe it gets that cold,' said Cairo, on the defensive.

Max pinched the bridge of his nose in a gesture of despair. 'You've got no idea, have you? If you're an example of your consultancy's planning, I dread to think what's going to happen when you're responsible for other people. On present form, you couldn't organise a day at the seaside, let alone a complex trip to one of the most inaccessible parts of the world!'

'Look, I'll be perfectly all right,' Cairo said crossly.

But as the hours passed, it got colder and colder. Earlier that day, as she had climbed up the furnace-like gorge, she had decided that what she wanted was to spend the rest of her life in the cold, but now she tossed and turned in an effort to get warm. This was an awful place! Everything was so extreme, and it was impossible to get comfortable. Every muscle in her body ached, and the fact that she was shivering didn't help.

If she turned on her side, she could see Max, warm and sound asleep in his sleeping bag, only a few feet away. It was all right for *him*, she thought resentfully, but she couldn't help wishing she had laid her mat a little closer. The darkness was so intense that every sound was magnified. She could hear Max breathing, and the mules shifting their hoofs among the stones. Mosquitoes whined annoyingly around her head and she pulled the sheet over her face, but that made her feel even more vulnerable. What if she didn't see all those snakes and scorpions creeping stealthily towards her?

Suddenly, the night was rent by a blood-curdling howl. Cairo sat bolt upright with a gasp, her heart pounding and her eyes wide and terrified. The howl was answered by another, and soon the darkness was filled with eerie yelping. How could Max sleep through it? She debated waking him up, but lost her nerve at the last minute. He would only be sarcastic. It was a wonder the sound of her teeth clacking like castanets hadn't woken him up already.

Cairo clutched the sheet around her. What was she doing here in this godforsaken place? Max was right. She should have found herself a proper job. She had been made to let Piers talk her into this crazy consultancy idea. She wanted to go home.

She was shaking with cold and fright. Too scared to get out of her sleep sheet, she leant over and managed to haul her rucksack towards her so that she could scrabble around for Max's shirt. Another layer might help.

'Can't you keep still?' Max demanded in sleepy irritation out of the darkness, making her jump. 'You've been thrashing around all night. The desert used to be a peaceful place before you came along.'

'*Peaceful*?' said Cairo bitterly between chattering teeth. 'How can you possibly call this . . . this *nightmare* of a place peaceful? I've had to put up with snoring, and mosquitoes dive-bombing me, all sorts of horrible creatures scuttling around on the ground and now werewolves howling for blood!'

'They're only jackals,' Max said with infuriating calm, and Cairo's voice rose to a squeak.

'*Jackals*? Wonderful!' She was teetering on the edge of hysteria. 'Not only are there millions of poisonous insects lining up to bite me, but I'm likely to be torn from limb to limb by a pack of scavenging jackals as well!'

'They're not interested in you,' said Max, exasperated. 'Scorpions and snakes will only attack in self-defence, so if you stay still you won't come to any harm.' He rolled back on to his side and closed his eyes once more. 'Just lie down and be quiet.'

Cairo lay back gingerly, but she was still freezing. She might as well put that shirt on now that she had got the pack. Sitting up once more, she began pulling things out of the top pocket. Where had she put it?

'What are you doing *now*?' Max sounded as if he was controlling his temper with an effort.

'I'm looking for your shirt,' she said sulkily.

'My shirt? Surely you're not cold?' His sarcasm was unmistakable and Cairo cast him a look of loathing.

'Yes, I am! You'll be delighted to know that I'm frozen, exhausted and scared stiff. I ache all over and I wish I'd never heard of you or your rotten desert!' She was struggling with the zip on the lower pocket. 'Why won't this——? Agh!'

Max sat up with a muttered exclamation. 'Now what?'

'I've broken a nail!' Cairo wailed, and burst into tears. It was the last straw.

Swearing fluently, Max disentangled himself from his sleeping bag and, after a wary shake for scorpions, thrust his feet into his shoes. He strode over to Cairo who was snuffling miserably into her sleep sheet, and picked her up bodily.

'What are you doing?' she spluttered, her flailing hands clutching instinctively round his neck and brushing against the warm skin of his shoulders. She was a tall girl, but he held her easily against his bare chest. She hadn't realised quite how strong he was.

'I am *trying* to get some sleep,' said Max distinctly, depositing her, sleep sheet and all, on his sleeping bag. 'And I'm not going to get any with you fussing and fidgeting away over there.' He threw her sleeping mat down beside his and moved her over as if she was a parcel. Then he unzipped his sleeping bag all the way round to make an eiderdown, lay down beside her, pulled her into the warmth of his body and threw the bag over both of them.

'If I'd known that tearing one of your nails was enough to break your spirit, I'd have broken one back at the camp,' he said.

Cairo found herself held against his hard body, enclosed by his arms. Her cheek was resting on his bare chest, and she was excruciatingly aware of the warm, matt texture of his skin. He had evidently been quite unmoved by carrying her scantily clad body close to his bare skin, but her heart was still thudding painfully against her ribs.

'My spirit isn't broken,' she said, rather muffled.

'Then why were you bawling your eyes out?'

'I wasn't bawling,' she said, trying to sound dignified. 'I was just . . . tired. I'm perfectly all right.'

Max loosened his hold on her. 'Oh, well, if you want to go back . . .'

'No,' said Cairo quickly. It felt safe and warm in his arms, and she didn't want to leave them. 'I mean, I don't want to disturb you again,' she added lamely.

'Good. In that case, will you please shut up and go to sleep?'

'I bet you say that to all the girls,' she muttered sourly, and felt rather than saw his reluctant smile above her head.

She was so cold that it took some time for the shivering to subside, but Max rubbed his hand rhythmically up and down her arm, and as his warmth seeped through her gradually her tired muscles began to relax. She could hear the steady, reassuring beat of his heart, and look over the broad chest at the still, black outlines of the rocks against the sky. Their silent looming presence no longer seemed threatening, and even the yippering jackals seemed to have faded away.

For the first time, Cairo noticed the stars. She had never seen so many. They crowded together, blurring the inky blackness of the sky with starlight. Why hadn't she seen how bright they were before?

She thought about Max, who must have stared up at them like this on countless nights. How remote her world must seem to him! Even after her world had fallen apart, she had still stayed in the city, where she felt at home. Max was right, Cairo admitted to herself. Her life was narrow. She could have claimed that London was a vast, cosmopolitan place, full of interest and activity, but, if she was honest with herself, her life was as limited as if she lived in a small village. She always went to the same places, saw the same people, they all lived in the same sort of houses. How long was it since she had met someone different? A few minutes' chat at a party, perhaps, but until she met Max she hadn't realised quite how restricted her experience had been.

For the first time, Cairo felt a pang of regret that she couldn't have met him under other circumstances. Lying in his arms, she felt as if all her senses were preternaturally heightened. Strange that a man who made no secret of his dislike of her could make her feel so safe. With the security of his body beside her, she felt as if she could see everything very clearly. Would things have been different if she had met Max in London? Would she have started to notice the shadows of the trees on the pavement, or the exuberance of the summer windowboxes, or the pink haze of a winter sunset over the Thames? Was the truth that she had never bothered to stop and look before because she knew they were there for free and had no exclusive cachet to make them worth her attention?

Cairo grimaced at the stars. She hadn't come to the desert for a course in self-knowledge. That was far too uncomfortable. She was here to do a job, even if it wasn't exactly what she had expected.

She smiled sleepily as she remembered how excited she had been when Piers had first proposed that they go into business together. 'We may not have qualifications,' he had said, 'but between us we've got loads of contacts. You've been jaunting around Europe for years; it'll be easy for you to set up social programmes, and even if we concentrate on the business angle you'll know lots of people who'll be able to point you in the right direction.'

Cairo had been enthused, lured by the glamorous picture of life Piers had painted for her. She had imagined herself jetting between Paris and Milan, perhaps running around Madrid with a clipboard, or coolly sorting out transport problems in Frankfurt. She had never dreamt that she would end up on top of a plateau in the Sahara, sleeping with a man she had only met for the first time yesterday, a man for whom she wasn't beautiful, capable Cairo Kingswood, but a thorough nuisance, and not a particularly attractive one at that. His heartbeat was slow and steady. *His* senses weren't careering out of control just because she was lying in his arms.

Unconsciously she sighed and nestled closer. At least she was warm and comfortable. Max was asleep. She could feel his chest rising and falling beneath her cheek, and she shifted slightly, so that her face was turned into the warmth of his throat. Her eyelashes feathered against his jaw and her lips were almost, *almost*, touching his skin. If she moved just a fraction, she would be able to taste him...

Cairo's eyes, which had been closing slowly, flicked open. What was she thinking of? This was *Max*.

But she was too tired to wonder what tricks her body was playing on her. She would just lie here quietly as

Max had instructed, and worry about it all tomorrow. Tomorrow she would be herself again, and there would be no strange yearnings to kiss the skin so tantalisingly close to hers.

Drifting in and out of consciousness, she felt Max stir in his sleep, and mumble something indistinct into her hair. It seemed the most natural thing in the world for Cairo to turn then, and press her lips to the pulse in his throat with a tiny sigh of release. She was vaguely aware of Max's arms tightening instinctively around her, and, giving herself up to a sense of infinite security, she slid at last into a deep sleep.

When Max shook her awake just before dawn, Cairo mumbled in protest and tried to draw the sleeping bag over her head.

'Leave me alone!'

The next moment, the comforting warmth of the bag was jerked away and Max was stirring her roughly with his foot. 'Come on, get up!'

Cairo struggled upright, rubbing her leaden eyes. 'It can't possibly be time to get up,' she yawned. 'I've only just gone to sleep.'

'If you'd spent less time making that appalling fuss last night, we might both have had a longer sleep,' Max pointed out, and she shifted uncomfortably, remembering how she had burst into tears over the broken nail. It wasn't like her to behave so hysterically.

'I wasn't myself last night, and you know it,' she said coldly.

'On the contrary,' said Max with an ironic look. 'I'd have said you were behaving quite in character, although even I didn't expect that a broken fingernail would provoke quite such a tragedy!'

Cairo flushed. 'It wasn't the nail. It was just the accumulation of events that got to me when I was tired, that's all.'

'What events?' Max asked with a glint of amusement. Last night's fire had been reduced to a circle of cold, white ashes, and he was busy setting up a small paraffin stove to boil some water. 'It was an ordinary, peaceful night in the desert. You were the only one creating a disturbance. I'd have thought if you could sleep in London you could sleep anywhere. You must be used to cars and sirens and pubs and televisions and people quarrelling next door all through the night. Last night should have been absolutely silent by comparison!'

'They were different sorts of noises,' Cairo said sulkily.

'Well, you'd better get used to them,' said Max, straightening, and regarding her with a complete lack of sympathy. If anything, he seemed to be positively enjoying her suffering, Cairo thought bitterly.

'Don't tell me,' she said. 'There's no five-star hotel to look forward to tonight, either.'

Unexpectedly Max grinned. 'Got it in one, Cairo! And since you will have noticed the lack of room service here, I suggest you get up and keep an eye on the stove while I go and have a word with the caretaker.'

Cairo eyed his back with resentment as he walked off. She didn't like the way he found her discomfort so amusing. If he had had any sense of decency, he would have been trying to make things easy for her instead of watching her with that mocking look in his eyes and making barbed comments about how out of place she was. She didn't like the way her heart lurched when he grinned either.

She had a rather uneasy memory of snuggling into his arms last night. She had been cold, of course, she reasoned, and it was natural to seek his body warmth. It had absolutely nothing to do with wanting to feel his arms around her or the solid strength of his body close to hers. She could remember looking up at the stars too, and being glad that she had met Max, and as for that bizarre compulsion to touch her lips to his skin . . . she must have been dreaming, or so tired that she had been delirious! Thank heaven Max had been asleep, or he would have got quite the wrong idea. Attractive he might be when he smiled, but he was just not the kind of man she would ever want to kiss!

CHAPTER FOUR

CAIRO extricated herself with some difficulty from her
tangled sleep sheet. A narrow strip of sky was just beginning to lighten over a line of weirdly shaped boulders
as she pulled on Max's shirt and buttoned it with chill
fingers. She had been too tired to behave normally last
night, but she had herself well under control again now.
She didn't care how ridiculous Max Falconer thought
her. She would never be able to turn herself into his ideal
woman, so she might as well carry on just as she was.

When Max came back, she was sitting crosslegged on
her sleeping mat, peering into a tiny handbag mirror as
she smoothed moisturiser over her face. 'I've made some
coffee,' she said without looking at him. 'The mug's over
there by the stove.'

After an incredulous stare when he noticed what she
was doing, Max picked up the mug with a grunt. 'I
thought I told you to leave all that stuff behind?'

'You did.'

'So you deliberately ignored my advice?'

'This isn't the Army, Max.' Cairo lowered the mirror
and looked up at him with truculent green eyes. 'You
gave me some advice, and I chose not to take it, that's
all. I'm quite capable of making my own decisions.
Contrary to what you think, I've got a perfectly good
mind of my own.'

'I haven't seen much evidence of it so far,' Max pointed
out.

Studiously ignoring him, Cairo finished moisturising
her face and began carefully applying sunblock.

'How many lotions do you need, for God's sake?' He
scowled down at her as he drank his coffee.

'I don't want to get sunburnt. You may be happy to have a skin like old leather, but I certainly don't intend to have one.'

'I sometimes wonder if you've appreciated just where you are, Cairo,' Max said in a tone of exasperated resignation. 'The paparazzi aren't up here waiting to jump out and take a snap of you not looking at your very best, so I hardly think you need to bother with full make-up!'

'I'm not putting on any make-up,' said Cairo, screwing the top back on the sunblock. 'I'm just taking care of my skin.'

'And in the meantime you expect me to stand here waiting patiently while you fuss over yourself?'

'I haven't noticed you being particularly patient,' she snapped. 'Surely it's not the end of the world if I spend five minutes giving myself a bit of protection. You'd be the first person to complain if I collapsed with sunstroke.'

Max chucked the dregs of the coffee away with an irritable gesture. 'Your hat's all the protection you should need. You don't seem to appreciate that I've got a job to do up here. I haven't got all day to hang around waiting for you.'

'I thought time "takes on a different meaning in the desert",' Cairo quoted him nastily as he glared at her.

'Believe me, it seems twice as long when it has to be spent with you! Now, hurry up!'

Cairo was still stiff and aching from yesterday's walk, and she grimaced as she hoisted the pack on to her back. Max had made her take another large container of water, as well as some food, and she staggered at first under the extra weight.

'I'll never be able to carry this!'

'If you can carry all those cosmetics as well as your Filofax, you can carry food and water that might well save your life,' said Max bluntly. 'If you want to leave something behind, I don't need to tell you what it should be!'

Cairo lapsed into sullen silence and plodded after him. After a while, her muscles loosened up with the renewed exercise, and as she got used to the weight on her back she began to look around her.

They were walking through a bizarre landscape of scattered boulders and vast pillars of rock, eroded by the wind into fantastic shapes. There was no path and Cairo couldn't help marvelling at how easily Max moved among the stones, always knowing exactly where he was going. He walked with a cat's deliberate, instinctive grace, never hesitating, never stumbling or puffing or puzzling over whether to go to the right or the left. He didn't seem to notice the heat. He just kept on walking with that sure tread, a quiet, capable figure that seemed part of, rather than intimidated by, the harsh surroundings.

Panting behind him, Cairo envied him his utter confidence. She was sure that she must look quite, quite alien out here. Still, the desert was somehow less threatening today. After the barren, looming gorge, this part of the plateau seemed full of life. 'It rained here about a month ago, for the first time in thirty years,' said Max when Cairo stopped to exclaim at a clump of brilliant yellow flowers growing out of bare rock. 'You're lucky to see it like this.'

After that, Cairo noticed clumps of flowers everywhere among the stones, and in the wadis, where the water had run, there were even great bushes of pink dog roses apparently thriving in the parched ground. Butterflies danced in the air, and for a few yards Cairo was accompanied by what looked suspiciously like a cabbage white, far from the English gardens where she was used to seeing them.

If only she hadn't been accompanied far more persistently by Max's disapproval, she might even have been enjoying herself, Cairo thought in some surprise as she followed his lean figure out of a narrow passage between the rocks and stopped in delight at the sight of a pale green field spread out before her.

'How lovely!' she exclaimed and walked forward with a smile, only to stare in horrified disbelief a moment later as the "grass" began to rise up around Max as he moved through it ahead of her.

Looking down, Cairo realised that she was standing at the edge of a carpet of insects, and she gave a strangled cry of revulsion as she clapped her hands to her eyes and took a rapid step backwards.

'What is it?' Max demanded impatiently, turning round.

'These ... these *things*!' she stammered in horror as she lowered her hands cautiously. 'What are they?'

'Locusts.' He cast a dispassionate eye over the swarm. 'They'll have started breeding with the rain. Looks like they might have the making of a plague here, doesn't it?'

'How can you be so casual about them?' Cairo cried. 'It's like some kind of horror story! They're absolutely revolting!'

'On the contrary,' said Max. 'The locals grill them on skewers as a delicacy.' He glanced at her and grinned. 'Want some for supper tonight?'

Cairo screwed up her face. 'Ugh, how disgusting!' She threw him a pleading look. 'Do we have to walk through them? Couldn't we go round?'

'No, we couldn't.' Max gestured at the carpet of insects stretching out towards the sides of the valley. 'It would take hours to find an alternative route, and I'm not going out of my way just because you can't cope with a few perfectly inoffensive creatures.'

'A few! There are millions of them!'

'Don't be so pathetic,' he said unsympathetically, setting off once more. 'Come on, they won't hurt you.'

'I can't!'

'Yes, you can,' he called over his shoulder. 'If you can deliberately strand yourself in the desert and climb that gorge without complaining, you can do this.'

Cairo looked after him in surprise. It was the nearest he had ever come to a compliment, and it was enough to make her screw up her courage and take a tentative step into the loathsome mass of insects. The baby locusts sprang out of the way of her feet and, disturbed, the older ones rose up with a whirr around her knees. She shuddered as they brushed against her bare legs. If only she had some trousers instead of these shorts!

Max had turned round and was watching her halting progress with a resigned expression. 'Hurry up!'

'I'm coming,' she snapped, and then cringed as one of the locusts flew up around her face. 'Ugh!'

Max sighed, exasperated. 'For heaven's sake!' He strode back towards her through the locusts and seized her hand, practically dragging her along with him. 'We'll never get anywhere at this rate.'

Cairo clung to him, pathetically grateful for the reassuring clasp of his fingers. His hand was strong and cool, calloused against the softness of her palm, and she focused on the feel of his fingers around hers as the locusts sprang and whirred around them.

She must have clutched at him, for he glanced down at her tense face. 'All right?' he asked.

Cairo nodded without speaking. She was staring straight ahead, concentrating on not looking down at the mass of insects around her feet.

'Poor Cairo; I don't suppose you counted on locusts when you planned this trip.'

At the unaccustomed note of sympathy in his voice, Cairo did look up. His expression held a strange mixture of exasperation, resignation and reluctant amusement, and the colour rose in her cheeks as her gaze dropped.

'I didn't count on any of it,' she admitted. She certainly hadn't counted on Max Falconer. 'You must be delighted.'

'Why?' Max sounded puzzled.

'Every time I make a fool of myself, you must think I'm just proving your point about how useless I am,' she said a little bitterly.

'Your trouble is that you're just not designed to survive somewhere like this,' said Max, not ungently. 'You've got that gloss of a creature made for luxury.'

'It doesn't take long for the gloss to wear off when you can't have a hot shower or wash your hair,' she sighed, and Max gave one of his unexpected, heart-shaking grins.

'This is obviously going to be a character-building experience for you, Cairo. Surviving swarms of locusts *and* not washing your hair for a few days. What greater test of character could a girl have?'

'I don't want my character built,' Cairo said, a shade sulkily, hating the fact that he was finding her loathing of these horrible insects so amusing. The air was filled with the strange click and hum of millions of wings, and, in spite of herself, her fingers tightened around Max's hand.

'I think you might find it getting built anyway,' said Max with some amusement. 'Still, if you think you don't need any help...' He made as if to release her hand, and Cairo gasped, clutching frantically at him.

'Don't let me go!'

She spoke instinctively, and regretted it as soon as the words were out of her mouth. They seemed to hang in the air, charged with hidden meaning. Max had raised one eyebrow, and Cairo met his gaze, her green eyes mute with appeal. 'I mean...please...?'

Max gave a strange, rather twisted smile and took a firm grip of her hand once more. 'Don't worry, Cairo, I'll keep good hold of you.'

They crossed the plain in silence. Cairo was humiliatingly aware of how pathetic he must think her, but she clung to his hand until at last the swarm thinned and then cleared. Once back on clear, stony ground, Max stopped and looked down at their linked hands.

'Are you OK now?'

'Yes.' Cairo's cheeks beneath her hat were scarlet. 'Thank you,' she muttered.

She felt stupidly lop-sided walking on her own without Max's fingers clasped impersonally around hers. He walked ahead of her, and she watched his back, trying to ignore the absurd tingling of her hand where he had held it.

She must pull herself together, Cairo scolded herself. She was supposed to be doing a job up here, not mooning along wishing Max was still holding her hand. She took her camera out in an effort to convince herself, and Max, how professional she was at heart, and took several shots as they went along to give Haydn Deane some idea of the scenery, but deep down she was beginning to think that Max was right. Now that she had climbed the plateau for herself, she could see that there was no way they could do a shoot up here. It would be impossible to get everyone up here, and, although she supposed she could hire some mules to carry up the equipment, she could just imagine how it would go down when she told the fashion team that they would have to sleep out with the jackals. They were used to five-star hotels, not a sleeping mat under the stars. Just like her.

Cairo looked around her at the dramatic rockscape and tried to visualise a shoot in progress. Expensive outfits on elegant girls, boxes of make-up, cameras, people with clipboards; they would all be bizarrely out of place, she realised. Max thought the same thing about her, she thought with an unconsciously wistful sigh.

Depressed at the thought that this whole nightmare trip might have been for nothing, Cairo trudged after Max. The worst thing was knowing that she couldn't just give up and go home. She would have to stick with him until he decided to go back down to the camp.

Max had stopped in the shade ahead and was waiting for her. Cairo had yet to get used to the fact that a landscape which consisted exclusively of rocks could be so varied. Sometimes it was flat and rubbly; at others they had to walk through narrow crevices between high rock walls. One minute they would be picking their way around enormous boulders, and the next crossing a plain studded with tall, thin pillars of rock, with huge round stones perched precariously on top, as if some giant had been amusing himself in seeing just how big a boulder he could balance on each narrow base.

Max was waiting below a massive outcrop that jutted out above his head. The cliffs here were fissured with crevices and narrow gulleys. Cairo glanced down them as she passed. Some disappeared into darkness, other opened out into a warren of rock passages and clearings.

Max's eyes narrowed slightly as he saw Cairo's dispirited expression. 'What's the matter?'

'Nothing,' Cairo sighed as she dropped into the shade, glad to escape the hammering sun. 'At least, nothing more than usual. I was just thinking how impossible it's going to be to organise a shoot up here.' She looked up at him, green eyes bright with a touch of her old defiance. 'Well, go on, say "I told you so"!'

Max squatted down beside her and pushed his hat back on his head. His cool eyes were light with amusement. 'I told you so,' he said obligingly.

Cairo shot him a sour look. 'I'll have to find some alternative locations, I suppose, but I can't do that while I'm stuck up here with you. When are you planning to go back down?'

'When I'm good and ready, Cairo, and not before,' said Max unhelpfully. 'You are, as you so graciously put it, stuck up here with me until I've finished what I came up here to do. I don't need to remind you that you weren't invited, do I?' The grey eyes looking into hers were implacable.

'No,' she muttered sullenly. 'I got myself into this, so now I'll just have to lump it.'

'I couldn't have put it better myself,' said Max with a grim smile as he straightened. 'I want to check out this area, so I'll leave you to feel sorry for yourself. You'll feel better about things after a rest, anyway. Stay here and, whatever you do, don't wander off where I can't find you again. I won't be that long.'

Cairo nodded dully and watched him disappear down one of the crevices, her mind already worrying away at the problem of what to do about a location for the shoot. She would have to be very careful not to set up any backs at Haydn Deane by telling them that the idea of using the plateau for a shoot was totally impractical. The best thing to do would be to come up with some alternatives and take back the arrangements as a *fait accompli*... but when was she going to have the time to do that? Max was quite capable of keeping her here for longer than he needed to just to teach her a lesson!

Somewhere in the distance, she could hear him whistling unconcernedly. It was all right for *him*. He didn't have to report back to Haydn Deane next week. Piers had grandly promised that she would come back with all the arrangements in place, and they were unlikely to be impressed if she turned up late with nothing to show for her recce but sore feet!

Cairo's mind circled fretfully around the problem until the timeless silence of the desert began to take effect. She couldn't do anything about it at the moment, she realised, and leant back against the cool stone. She wondered what Max was doing. He must be delighted that she had had to accept that he had been right in the first place. Still, some men would have crowed a lot more, Cairo admitted fairly. He had been much nicer today, now she came to think about it. Once or twice she had surprised that amused look in his eyes, and he really looked quite different when he smiled...

There was something reassuringly capable about him, too. He had kept her warm last night, and helped her through all those horrible locusts, although he could just have easily told her that she would have to cope by herself. He had been pretty dour yesterday, but it wasn't surprising that he hadn't welcomed the idea of some hopeless female foisting herself upon him, Cairo went on to herself in large-minded spirit. She had been argumentative too. No wonder he had been so grumpy. It wasn't his fault she had made such a rash decision. From now on she would be quiet and accommodating, and perhaps he might realise that she had learnt her lesson and change his mind about staying on the plateau.

It was very quiet. Cairo sat quite still, speculating about Max and whether, if she got to know him any better, he would turn out to be much nicer than she had given him credit for up to now, until, like a cold trickle running down her neck she realised she hadn't heard Max's whistle for some time.

She glanced at her watch. She had been sitting here for nearly an hour. Surely he should have been back by now? The silence seemed to intensify until it was like a dead weight, and she got to her feet in a sudden rush of panic.

'Max?' she called in a thin, high voice, but the only answer was a deep, mocking silence. 'Max?' she called again, more urgently this time.

Nothing.

She forced herself to wait for five more minutes while her heart thudded apprehensively. She had never felt so alone; even the butterflies seemed to have deserted her. She wouldn't even have minded seeing a locust right then. At least it would prove that she wasn't the only creature alive on the planet. Her ears strained to hear some indication that Max was near by, but the harder she listened, the more deafening the silence became.

When the five minutes were up, she moved hesitantly towards the crevice where Max had vanished. He had told her to stay where she was, but what if something had happened to him?

Cairo peered down the crevice and called his name once more. It echoed eerily off the rock, and she shivered in spite of the heat. The thought of disappearing into an opening like this was all too reminiscent of the horror films she had seen where the heroine went off on her own. Cairo had always groaned and knew she would *never* be that stupid.

'Oh, pull yourself together,' she snapped out loud and stepped cautiously into the crevice. Max might be lying hurt while she dithered around out here.

It was dark and narrow inside, but she felt her way gingerly through to the far side where she came out suddenly into a blaze of light. She found herself in a large well, strewn with boulders. A number of passageways led off from the sheer cliffs that rose up all around. Max might be down any of them!

Cairo pressed her hands to her cheeks and tried to think sensibly. She mustn't panic! She moved warily into the light just as Max materialised from a cleft in the rock.

'What are you doing here?' he demanded behind her.

Cairo's nerves were so taut that she screamed and spun around, both hands clasped to her throat, green eyes wide with shock.

Max raised an irritable eyebrow. He looked solid and distinct against the pale rock and his hat was tilted back on his head. 'What on earth's the matter with you?'

'You startled me,' she gasped. Her heart was hammering so hard she could hardly breathe.

'You shouldn't be wandering around here,' Max said sternly. 'I told you to stay where you were. Can't you ever do as you're told?' The lightness of his grey-green eyes unsettled Cairo every time. They were so unexpected in that severe, sunburnt face. It wasn't even as if he was particularly handsome. The angular planes of his face were too hard, the line of mouth and jaw too uncompromising. There were creases at the edges of his eyes, as if he had spent too many years narrowing his gaze against the glare.

Suddenly realising that she was staring, Cairo wrenched her eyes away from his face, embarrassed to realise how joyful she was to see him again. 'I came to look for you,' she explained awkwardly. 'You'd been gone so long, I thought something might have happened to you.'

'I'm quite capable of looking after myself,' he said ungratefully. 'Which is more than I can say for you. You could easily have got lost wandering around these crevices. In future, please do as you're told and stay where I can find you.'

'Well, when you're trapped somewhere with a broken leg, don't expect *me* to come and find you!' Cairo snapped, quite forgetting her earlier appreciation of how difficult she had made things for Max and her resolve not to aggravate him any more. 'I won't waste any effort worrying about you in future!'

'There's no need to get on your high horse,' Max retorted. 'If you bothered to think at all, you'd realise that I'm merely concerned about *your* safety.'

They glared at each other, tight-lipped, until Max took off his hat, ran his fingers through his hair in a gesture of exasperation, and jammed the hat back on his head with a sigh. 'Since you're here, you might as well come and see what I've found.'

He led her down the cleft to another, smaller clearing. 'Look over there,' he said, pointing towards an overhanging rock. It sheltered a series of primitive rock paintings done in ochre. Hunters, women and children, giraffe and cattle and dogs and abstract figures covered the rock, sometimes overlapping each other.

Cairo stood silently before them, marvelling that such simple lines could be so expressive of life and movement. 'Who painted this?' she asked at last.

'We don't really know,' said Max quietly. The brittle tension between them had subsided as quickly as it had exploded, and they stood close together, awed by the vivid images of a vanished past. 'The Sahara used to be a much more fertile place,' he went on. 'We assume that there were nomadic tribes who passed through here thousands of years ago, but we don't know for sure.' He pointed towards a painting of a man clearly running with a spear. 'It looks as if they were hunters, but these paintings are almost all they left behind. You can find them all over the plateau. Most of them are still to be discovered; I only came across these by accident.'

It gave Cairo a strange feeling to be standing there with Max, knowing that they were probably the first people to see those paintings for thousands of years. Her gaze lingered on a woman bending protectively over a child in an age-old gesture. She found it surprisingly moving.

'Some things never change, do they?' she said, almost to herself. 'The people who painted these lived totally different lives, but they must have been just like us, loving each other, loving their children.' She leant forward to look more closely at the graceful figure. 'This woman is thousands of years old, but she and I are just the same.'

Max eyed her with a glint of amusement. 'I don't imagine *she* refused to move without her personal organiser, or was allowed to spend hours on her beauty routine every day!'

'That wasn't what I meant,' said Cairo, trying to sound frosty, but unable to prevent a reluctant smile tugging at her mouth. 'As far as the important things in life go, we would have had lots in common,' she added, more seriously.

'Oh, yes?' Max was patently unconvinced.

'I was a child like everyone else,' she insisted. 'You can tell from these paintings that those people loved their children, just like my parents loved me. And one day,

I'd like to get married and have children that I could love just as that woman must have loved her child.'

'Funny, I wouldn't have put you down as a maternal type,' said Max with a curious look. He stuck his hands in his pockets and studied her dispassionately. 'No, I'd have thought you'd think of a baby as a designer accessory and hand it over to a nanny so that you could make yourself up in peace.'

Cairo looked back at the woman bending over her child, and her face softened. 'No, I'd love to have children,' she said, unconsciously wistful.

'It should be easy enough for a girl like you to find a husband, surely?'

Cairo thought of the men she had been out with. They had been attractive and charming, but somehow she had never been able to rid herself of the notion that they might not have been so attentive if her father had not been quite so rich. After the scandal broke, there had been a lot fewer invitations. She sighed. 'Perhaps I'm just choosy.'

'Or waiting for someone rich enough?' Max's voice was harsh.

She looked up at him, her eyes very clear and green beneath her hat. 'I'm waiting for someone who really loves me,' she said.

There was an odd little silence. Cairo was very conscious of Max standing beside her, looking down into her eyes with a peculiar expression in his own. If she lifted her hand, she would be able to touch him, and with the thought came an urge to take a step closer and lean against his broad chest and listen to his heart beating. It was so strong that for one appalled moment, she thought that she had swayed towards him, and she jerked her gaze away, almost stumbling as she stepped back.

They spent that night in a sheltered gully. There were shallow caves at the bottom of the cliffs, all carpeted with drifts of sand, as soft and white as talcum powder, and glittering in the last slanting rays of the sun.

Cairo was unusually silent. She felt awkwardly nervous, as gauche as any teenager. She was terrified of meeting Max's eyes in case he could read the sudden, inexplicable desire that had seized her. It didn't make any sense. She didn't even *like* the man! Why did her pulse thump insistently at the mere thought of his mouth, his hands? Why did her skin burn whenever she remembered how it had felt to be held in his arms?

She ought to be thinking about Haydn Deane, she told herself feverishly. She should be worrying about what she would tell her father if this trip was the disaster it was shaping up to be, but all she could think about was Max and whether she would share his sleeping bag again tonight.

Her stomach churned at the prospect. She didn't know whether she longed to lie beside him, or whether she was terrified at the risk that her body might betray her.

Max seemed preoccupied too, and the long silences between them jangled with tension. Why was her body doing this? Cairo wondered helplessly, watching him light the paraffin stove. His trousers were stretched over the taut muscles of his thighs as he hunkered down by the stove, and she could see the line of his spine through his faded shirt. She wondered how he would react if she ran her finger down it, and her heart knocked nervously against her ribs at the idea.

He was just an ordinary man, she told herself desperately. She just happened to be in an extraordinary situation with him. That was all. In a few days, they would be back to normality, and they would both be only too glad to say goodbye to each other. Cairo let the sand trickle slowly through her fingers. How long had she known Max? Three days, was that all? Already it was impossible to imagine never seeing him again.

The heat evaporated into the clear air as darkness fell. Cairo did her best to behave normally and make conversation as they ate the simple meal of soup and chewy bread, but it was hopeless. Max seemed to have lapsed back into bad temper, and made no effort to keep the conversation going. Her voice sounded brittle and her sentences kept trailing off into a taut silence.

They shared the mug of coffee as they had the night before. Whenever their hands touched, a current of electricity seemed to flow between them, and Cairo would gulp at the hot coffee, burning her tongue. In the end, she decided that she would just have to broach the subject of where she would sleep herself. Max obviously wasn't going to help her.

'I should have brought a sleeping bag with me,' she began nervously.

Max shrugged. 'It would have been more sensible, but you can't do anything about it now. You'll just have to carry on sharing mine.'

'I'm sorry,' she said. 'It makes it rather awkward.'

'What's awkward about it?'

'Well ... sleeping together.'

'It doesn't bother me,' said Max brusquely. 'Sleeping is the operative word, after all. If you think I'm having trouble containing my animal lusts, you can stop worrying. Girls like you just don't interest me.'

'Girls like you just don't interest me'.

Cairo stiffened as the sense of recognition that had nagged at her ever since she had first met Max clicked suddenly into place, and she sat bolt upright, staring at him incredulously. How could she have forgotten? She should have known as soon as he kissed her!

Max frowned at her expression. 'What is it?'

'I *do* know you,' she said slowly. 'I thought I did. You're Davina Fothergill's son.'

When she was younger, Davina had been a celebrated hostess, famed for her beauty, her parties and her succession of wealthy husbands. Gerald Falconer had been her first, Cairo remembered now. He had also been the richest, but, after Davina had left him and their two children for a man more prepared to indulge her jet-set pretensions, he had become more and more reclusive. She hadn't heard his name mentioned in years.

'It is you, isn't it?' she asked, when Max didn't say anything.

He swilled the coffee dregs around the mug before chucking them away on to the ground. 'It's not the way I think of myself, but yes, she is my mother,' he said with a bitter edge to his voice. He wasn't looking at Cairo. 'You're out of date, though. I believe she calls herself Mrs Kellerman now.'

That was right. Cairo remembered there had been a splash in the gossip pages a couple of months ago when Davina had got married for the sixth time, looking as glamorous as ever. It was hard to believe that she had a son as old as Max, but Cairo knew that it was true. She remembered meeting him.

She looked at him out of the corner of her eye. Did *he* remember? She hoped not.

It had been New Year's Eve, about ten years ago. Davina, married to her fourth husband by then, had thrown a huge party and invited a glittering array of the rich and famous. Jeremy Kingswood had taken his adored daughter. At sixteen, Cairo was just learning how to use her undoubted good looks, and had enjoyed herself enormously flirting with all the men. Only one had remained impervious to her charm.

'Who's that?' Cairo whispered to her friend, Emily.
'Who?'
'The guy standing next to Phil over there. The one who looks completely uninterested in anyone.' Even in his early twenties, Max had had a remote quality that had set him apart from the hectic gaiety around him.

'That's Davina's son, Max,' Emily told her. 'Davina usually ignores her children, but she's playing at being a mother this Christmas. It's part of her new image. I think Max would rather have stayed with his father, but his sister likes being with Davina and she made him come and play at happy families. He looks as if he'd rather be anywhere but here, doesn't he?'

Cairo was intrigued by Max's air of cool inaccessibility and, flown with her first taste of success at this glamorous, adult party, she made a giggly bet with Emily that she would get him to kiss her before the night was out.

With all the confidence of a pretty sixteen-year-old, she set out to charm him, but Max ignored her inviting smiles and looks, and was patently uninterested in her chatter. Piqued, Cairo was determined to win her bet. As the party revved up towards midnight, she saw him slip outside on to the long terrace, and, grabbing a piece of mistletoe, she followed him through the French windows.

He was standing by the balustrade, with his hands in his pockets, looking out over the frosty gardens. The severity of the black dinner-jacket and tie suited him, and the moonlight threw the lines of his face into austere relief.

Cairo strolled up to him with studied casualness. 'All alone?'

Max closed his eyes briefly and a nerve hammered in his jaw. 'As you see,' he said between clenched teeth.

'Wouldn't you like some company to see the new year in?' asked Cairo with what was meant to be a seductive smile.

'Frankly, no.' Max swung round to face her. 'Since you seem to be too stupid to take a hint, I'll make it as clear as I can. I'm not interested in girls like you. I prefer a more sophisticated technique.'

Cairo's green cat eyes narrowed. She had been pampered and adored all her life, and she wasn't used to being spoken to like that. She didn't like it one bit, but she was too used to getting her own way to give up without a fight. She had made a bet with Emily, and she was determined to win it.

'Don't I even get a kiss for New Year?' she said, spinning the mistletoe provocatively between her fingers.

'Is that what it will take to get rid of you?' Max reached out without warning and jerked her towards him. His fingers dug cruelly into her bare arms, and suddenly Cairo was frightened.

'Let me go!'

'No. You wanted a kiss,' he said as he bent his head. 'Now you're going to get one.'

Cairo's experience of school dances hadn't prepared her for a kiss like that. Max's mouth was cool and ruthless, and Cairo felt the ground rock beneath her feet, discovering too late that she had been playing a dangerous game. Max was no schoolboy, and she was shattered by an explosion of conflicting emotions when he dropped her rudely down to earth.

'There,' he said coolly, putting her away from him. 'You've had your kiss. Now run along and practise your technique on someone who doesn't mind spoilt, silly little girls.'

Cheeks burning with humiliation, Cairo had fled.

Now, as the memory swept back all too vividly, she felt her face grow hot once more, and she was glad of the darkness so that Max couldn't see her too clearly.

'You probably don't remember me,' she said lightly, hoping desperately that it was true. 'We met at a party once.'

Max turned his head, and his piercing eyes gleamed in the moonlight. 'I remember you all right,' he said. 'You were the girl who was determined to have what she wanted. You haven't changed that much.'

Cairo bit her lip at the sardonic note in his voice. 'Why didn't you say if you recognised me?'

'You didn't remember. Why should I remind you of an incident that wasn't particularly enjoyable for either of us?'

If only she could forget again! Cairo felt all the rage and humiliation and deep, secret excitement that she had felt at sixteen as she had rushed away from him. All the time she had been trying to be cool and businesslike, he had been remembering her as an adolescent! No wonder he had been so contemptuous!

She tried to carry her embarrassment off with a laugh. 'Do you know, I'd forgotten all about that kiss!' She had been so humiliated that she had deliberately wiped it from her memory. 'It was all very silly, wasn't it?'

'Very,' Max agreed. 'I hope you didn't make a practice of throwing yourself at every man like that?'

Cairo's fists clenched. He wasn't making it any easier for her! 'As a matter of fact, it was just a silly bet I had with a friend. It wasn't anything to do with you.'

She had hoped to sound cutting, but Max was unperturbed. 'So you won your bet?'

Cairo hesitated. 'No,' she said at last. 'No, I didn't.' She hadn't wanted anyone to know about that kiss. 'I didn't tell her. I just pretended you'd gone.'

'I see.' Max's uncomfortably penetrating eyes rested on her profile. 'Well, that explains your attention, anyway. I didn't think I was your type.'

'You weren't,' she said shortly.

'If I'm not your type, what is?' he asked in a mocking tone.

Cairo thought about touching her lips to his throat last night. She thought about the strength in his arms, and the warmth of his body and the heart-clenching set of his mouth. Then she pushed those thoughts firmly aside. She wasn't going to be humiliated a second time!

'If I said the complete opposite of you, that ought to give you some idea of the kind of man I like,' she said. Out of the edge of her eyes, she could see his mouth curl in quiet amusement, and her chin tilted. 'What about you? What type of girls do you like?'

Max stretched his long legs out before him, and leant back against the sand, linking his arms behind his head. 'A girl who isn't a type,' he said. 'A girl who's just herself.'

Cairo felt her heart twist with jealousy. 'Who is this paragon?'

'I'm not sure that she exists,' said Max with an edge of bitterness, and she wondered how cynical his beautiful, faithless mother had made him.

'If she does, you're not going to meet her stuck out in the middle of the desert,' said Cairo, more sharply than she had intended.

Max looked up at the still desert night. 'I might,' he said.

Cairo spent ages getting ready for bed. She spun out cleaning her face and brushing her teeth and packing everything away as long as she could in the vain hope that Max might have fallen asleep before she got there, but at last she could put off lying down beside him no longer. She kept thinking about Max, about how he had been then and the man he was now. He had broadened out, become tougher, harder, and the remote quality that she had first noticed had intensified into that distinctive self-sufficiency. But his eyes were the same, and he had the same devastating ability to make her feel edgy and unsettled.

Lifting her side of the sleeping bag, Cairo slid beneath it and lay rigidly at the very edge of her mat, but it was so narrow that she was still bare inches away from Max. She tried to wriggle into a more comfortable position, just as he shifted on his mat, and their arms brushed inadvertently. Cairo flinched away as if she'd been stung.

'What are you so tense about?' asked Max testily.

'Nothing. I just don't find sleeping like this particularly comfortable.'

'Does it bother you that you once asked me to kiss you?'

'Of course not!' Cairo gave an unconvincing laugh. 'I'm hardly likely to be bothered by the memory of a silly little kiss like that!'

Max propped himself up on one elbow to look down into her face. 'What sort of kiss would bother you?'

'None!'

'I don't believe that,' he said softly, leaning over to lift a strand of hair from her cheek. 'I've kissed you twice now, remember?'

The breath dried in Cairo's throat as her heart slowed to a painful, irregular thud. 'I'd prefer to forget,' she managed through stiff lips.

'Would you?' Max leant closer until his mouth was almost touching hers. Cairo was mesmerised by his eyes. She wanted to look away, but she was held, helpless beneath him. His body was tantalisingly close, and she ached with a dark, desperate need.

'Would you?' he whispered again against her lips, and Cairo's hands lifted of their own accord and slid instinctively up his arms and over the muscles in his shoulders, luxuriating in the feel of the warm, smooth skin that covered such steely strength.

Low in her throat, she murmured what might have been a protest, but as Max's mouth found hers at last it was swept away by a tide of sheer desire. Her arms tightened, pulling him closer so that his body crushed her slenderness, and her lips opened eagerly to his questing tongue. His mouth was warm, insistent. Dimly she realised that this was what she had been thinking about all day: Max's kiss, deep and demanding, and his hands hard against her skin. He had slipped beneath her T-shirt, and she quivered beneath his touch as his fingers burned over the silken length of her thigh.

Excitement was crackling along her senses, and when Max lifted his head abruptly, she gasped for breath. He was breathing hard too, but the suddenly shuttered expression in his eyes shocked her back to devastating reality. Her arms dropped from his neck.

'I-I thought you weren't interested in girls like me,' she said shakily, moistening her lips with her tongue.

'I'm not,' said Max. 'Let's just say that I was interested to see whether your technique had improved.' His gaze rested on her mouth for a moment. 'It has.' Then he rolled back to his mat and straightened the sleeping bag over them both as if nothing had happened.

Cairo couldn't speak. She was shaking with reaction, her body burning with rage and humiliation and un-satisfied desire. She turned her back on him so that he wouldn't see the devastation on her face, but pride came to her rescue at last.

'Yours hasn't,' she said, but she knew that she lied.

CHAPTER FIVE

RIGID with humiliation, her body still throbbing with treacherous need, Cairo expected to lie awake all night, but in the end she fell into a deep sleep brought on by sheer exhaustion.

She stirred as the first rays of the sun fell across her face. Opening her eyes slowly, she blinked. The air was suffused with a soft purply-gold light, and for a moment she lay contentedly, aware only of the deep silence and strangely haunting beauty of the place, but, as sleep dissolved, memory seeped back, and she stiffened.

She was lying on her side, staring at rock pillars that guarded the entrance to the gully where they had slept. She could sense Max lying still beside her, and very cautiously, she turned her head to see if he was still asleep.

He lay on his stomach, his face turned towards her. Cairo's mouth twisted as her gaze rested on his sleeping figure. The muscles in the powerful shoulders were relaxed, but she could recall only too vividly the feel of their strength beneath her fingers. In sleep, his face looked younger, less hard, and his mouth was slightly curved, as if he smiled while he dreamt.

Cairo's stomach clenched, remembered how its touch had devastated all her defences. How was she going to face him this morning, with his kiss still strumming along her senses? Easing herself out from her sleep sheet, she slipped on her shoes. She didn't want to risk waking him by getting fully dressed, so she crept to the entrance of the gully, still in the long T-shirt she had slept in. She just needed to be alone for a while.

Below the rock pillars, she hesitated. Facing her was what looked like an almost identical gorge. If she walked down there for a while, she wouldn't get lost, and it would be easy to find her way back to Max.

Max. The early morning light threw the texture of the rocks into patterns of pink and gold, and softened the shadows to blue, but Cairo barely noticed. She had wanted to be alone, but the memory of Max was so vivid that he might as well have been walking beside her, his hand on her thigh, his mouth against hers.

Cairo walked more quickly, trying to shake off the memories. She would pretend nothing had happened. If he thought she was going to make a big scene, he would soon discover his mistake. She would be icily polite when required, but ignore him for the rest of the time, and with any luck *he* would be the one to feel ashamed.

The gorge twisted slightly, and without warning dropped away into a steep slope, covered with rocks and rubble. Wrapped in her thoughts, Cairo slithered and scrambled down. The last bit was a sheer drop down eight feet or so, but she swung herself down from a boulder without thinking, so intent was she on how to show Max that his kisses didn't matter to her in the least.

The morning air was clear and fresh, and she began to feel calmer as she walked on. She had been letting Max and this eerily beautiful plateau get to her. It wasn't like her to get so worked up about a couple of kisses, she who had always prided herself on her cool sophistication! Well, it wouldn't happen again. All she had to do was get through the next couple of days, and then she could put Max Falconer out of her mind once and for all.

Deciding that she was more than capable of facing him now, Cairo turned and made her way back along the gorge, and it was only when she reached the steep drop she had jumped down so carelessly that she realised that getting back to Max was not going to be as easy as she had thought.

She bit her lip as she looked up at the boulder wedged about halfway up the sheer slope. It was just too high for her to climb up to, and its smooth sides offered no hold if she tried to jump. Cairo walked carefully along the bottom of the slope, looking for some other way to climb out, but it was hopeless, she realised in consternation. It had been such a little drop on the way down, but now the rock seemed as sheer and unscalable as a wall of glass.

If she could just get up on to that boulder, she would be able to haul herself the rest of the way. Cairo tried a few futile jumps, and then launched herself at the wall, but there wasn't so much as tiny crevice to dig her fingers into, and her feet scrabbled helplessly against the smooth rock.

Gasping for breath, she stepped back. This was ridiculous. It wasn't as if she was stuck at the bottom of an abyss. All she had to do was climb a few feet. There *must* be a way!

She wondered whether Max was awake, whether he had missed her yet. Would he come looking for her? The very thought of him was steadying. Cairo took a deep breath and jumped again for the boulder, but as she fell back, she stumbled and twisted her ankle badly beneath her. She cried out as she felt the wrench, and for a minute could only sit in the dust, biting her lip hard until the pain subsided to an ache.

She hadn't broken it, anyway, she thought, stretching her leg out gingerly to examine her ankle. It was just a sprain, but it hurt vilely. She would never get up that rock now, she thought in rising panic. How could she have been that stupid?

Stupid, thoughtless, criminally careless. It was nothing to what Max would say to her when he found her. *If* he found her.

Cairo struggled awkwardly to her feet, wincing as her sprained ankle touched the ground. 'Max!' she called. 'Max!' She could hear her voice echoing off the walls of the gorge. The emptiness of the sound chilled her before, incredibly, there was an answer, faint and disembodied in the distance.

'Cairo?'

'I'm here,' she called, almost sobbing with relief.

A couple of minutes later, Max appeared at the top of the slope, and Cairo's world, which had been rocking as the full realisation of her danger hit her, steadied abruptly at the sight of him. From below, he was silhouetted against the sky, and she couldn't see his expression properly, but it was clear that he was livid. Cairo didn't care. He was there, and she was safe.

'What are you doing down there?' he asked furiously. 'Do you realise how long I've been looking for you?'

'I just wanted a walk,' said Cairo. 'It didn't seem too difficult to get down, but now I can't get back up again, and I've twisted my ankle.'

'I hope it hurts,' Max said savagely, relief at finding her merely fanning the flames of his anger. 'I've *told* you about wandering off on your own, but do you listen? No! Anyone else would have learnt by now that the plateau is a dangerous place, but not Cairo Kingswood! No, she just gets out of bed and strolls off, without letting me know that she's going at all, let alone where! I don't suppose it occurred to you to wonder how I might feel waking up to find you gone?'

If anything, she would have thought he'd be glad, Cairo thought, but she didn't want to provoke him any further. 'I'm sorry,' she said meekly.

'One of these days you're going to find that it's too late to be sorry. If I had any sense I'd leave you down there and teach you a lesson!' said Max, refusing to be placated, but he negotiated his way down the stony slope with care and then lowered himself over the tip to the boulder Cairo had been trying to reach.

Lying on his front, he stretched his hands down towards her. 'If you can get hold of my hands, I'll pull you up.'

It took a couple of attempts, but at last Cairo managed to grab hold of him and feel the strength flowing through his hands. Red-faced with effort, he hauled her slowly upwards, while she braced herself against the rock with her good foot until she was able to collapse into an untidy heap against the hard comfort of his body. For a long moment, nothing could be heard but their wheezing as they tried to get their breath back, then, suddenly aware of the T-shirt rucked up to her thighs, Cairo pulled it down awkwardly and struggled upright, unable to prevent a gasp of pain as her injured leg took her weight.

'Let me see,' Max ordered. He took her foot in a firm grasp, and although his probing fingers were unexpectedly gentle, his expression was grim as he let her go. 'Twisted,' he confirmed. 'Which means that you've become even more of a liability than you were before, if that's possible.' He got to his feet carefully in the limited space. 'I don't think I've ever met anyone capable of being as stupid, selfish and totally irresponsible as you, Cairo,' he said in a cold, quiet voice, and she quailed, even though she recognised dimly that much of his anger stemmed from the after-effects of fear for her. 'You forced me to bring you up here, you've slowed me down and distracted me from my work, and now, when we're a whole day from the camp and we're running low on food and water, you go and sprain your ankle because you're too self-centred and stupid to listen to my advice about your own safety! I suppose you realise that if it hadn't been for you, I could have finished here today and started back to the camp? Now we're going to have to wait until that swelling goes down and you can walk again.'

'I can walk today,' said Cairo in a small voice. He was right. She had thought only of herself. She had been just as selfish and arrogant as he said. 'I just need to strap it up.'

'Don't be even more stupid than you've shown yourself to be already! You can't go anywhere on that ankle today.' Max took her arm roughly and pulled her up from the boulder, continuing to harangue her as he half led, half dragged her up the slope.

Cairo bit down on her lip to keep from crying out as she limped behind him, but the stones underfoot kept skidding beneath their feet, and she was almost at the top when she slipped and would have fallen down to the bottom again if Max's grip had not held her. Her weight pulled him off balance; he stumbled but managed to save himself by grabbing at the stones with his free hand before he could slide back.

Cairo saw his hand slip between two stones, dislodging them, and heard a sharp, indrawn breath that was somehow more chilling than a cry of agony.

'Max?' She clutched at his arm with both her hands as his face went grey and he sank to his knees, holding his wrist. 'Max, what is it?'

The muscles in his neck were standing out like cords as he fought the pain. 'Bitten,' he managed to say with enormous effort. 'See what it was.'

Cairo looked around frantically, and her horrified eyes fell on the tail-end of a snake slithering away between the rocks. Her involuntary recoil dislodged a shower of small stones which slid down and fell over the drop. 'Max, we've got to get off this slope,' she said urgently. 'Can you move?'

Later, Cairo never knew how they managed to make it the last few feet to the top of the slope, and Max buckled at the top. Ignoring the pain in her ankle, she dragged him over to the deep, cool shade of a rocky outcrop and dropped to her knees beside him. His lips were drawn back in a terrifying grimace of pain as he leant back against the rock, and his temples were wet with sweat. He was clutching his hand protectively to his chest, and when she leant over, she could see the two ugly puncture marks.

'Did you see what it was?' he croaked. 'Any markings?'

She shook her head. 'It was a snake, but I just saw the tail, not enough to describe it.'

Max closed his eyes. 'Have to wait and see,' he muttered. 'Don't know how poisonous.'

Cairo was terrified by his appearance, but she forced herself to sound calm. 'Max, I'm going to get the first-aid kit from your rucksack,' she said clearly, hoping he could hear her. 'Keep as still as you can until I get back.' His eyes were still tightly closed, but he managed a nod, and she touched his hair in a fleeting gesture of reassurance. 'I won't be long,' she promised.

She limped back down the gorge as fast as she could. Every step jarred her ankle, but she clenched her teeth and wouldn't let herself rest. She couldn't believe how far she had walked without noticing it. It would take her ages to get back to Max at this rate. If only she could go a bit faster. If only she hadn't twisted her ankle. If only she hadn't set out on that wretched walk at all!

Cairo's face was white and set by the time she made it back to where they had camped. Max's rucksack was already packed up, his sleeping mat rolled and strapped on top, and she decided to take it all. There was no question of moving Max, so she would just have to make him as comfortable as she could. She could come and get her own stuff later.

She was desperate to get back to him, but forced herself to strap up her ankle first. She would be able to make better time if she had some support, she realised, and dressed awkwardly before struggling to hoist his pack on to her back.

Bent double by its weight, and limping heavily, it was only force of will that got Cairo back along the gorge. Later, when she tried to pick up the pack, she simply couldn't do it, but at the time, with the vision of Max lying there in agony, she simply blocked out everything but the need to get back to him as soon as possible.

He was lying so still when Cairo got back that for one heart-wrenching moment she thought he was dead. 'No!'

she whispered, as the world went black, but then he moved his head, and she fell to her knees beside him, careless of the pain that jolted up from her ankle. 'Max! Oh, Max! Can you hear me?'

With tremendous difficulty, he opened his eyes and looked into her face. 'You came back,' he mumbled.

'I'm sorry I was so long. I couldn't go very fast.' Cairo fumbled with the lid of the water bottle and held it to his lips so that he could drink. Then she found the flannel, splashed water over it with an unsteady hand, and wiped his face and neck. She didn't know if it helped at all, but she was desperate to do something. His lips were white and pressed firmly together. 'How do you feel?' she asked, hoping her voice didn't reveal the stark terror that she felt.

'Alive,' he whispered, and, in spite of the pain, a tiny smile touched the corners of his mouth. 'That's a good sign. If it had been any of the snakes I was worried about, I'd have been dead by now.'

Cairo examined the first-aid kit, her hands shaking with exhaustion and fear. There was no anti-snake serum, but she found some penicillin tablets and made him take four. Unrolling the sleeping mat, she managed to haul and push Max on to it and tucked the sleeping bag around him. He was very drowsy and sweating profusely, and his eyes were unfocused when she lifted the lids.

Why was she so useless? Max had been right; she just wasn't capable of dealing with an environment as alien as this one. She had read a book on desert survival before she left, and there had been a whole section on how to deal with bites and stings, but it was a complete blank now. All she could remember was that she had to keep his arm as still as possible. Cairo sat back, being careful not to jar her ankle, and tried to think. What she needed was some kind of splint. A search back along the gorge revealed some dead, sun-bleached branches of an ancient acacia tree which for some mysterious reason had chosen to grow in this inhospitable spot. She chose the straightest and smoothest for the splint and gathered the others for a fire that evening.

'Do you know what you're doing?' Max asked in a weak voice as she crouched beside him and began bandaging his arm with much more confidence than she felt.

Reassure the patient, Cairo remembered. 'Oh, yes,' she said breezily. 'I've done a first-aid course.'

'Really?'

She looked down into his face and faltered. The grey-green eyes were clouded with pain but managed to glint with more than a touch of scepticism.

'Well, no,' she confessed. 'I thought it would make you feel better if you thought I was confident. I'm just using my common sense.'

'I didn't know you had any of that,' Max whispered, but a taut smile lifted the corners of his mouth once more.

'I haven't given you much reason to think so, have I?' she said, and bowed her head over her bandaging, overcome with remorse.

His good hand reached across and touched hers. 'I'm sorry I shouted at you, Cairo,' he said with difficulty. 'I was so afraid I'd never find you, and then there you were suddenly. I don't know why, I just lost my temper...'

His voice died away, and Cairo clasped his hand in instinctive reassurance. 'It's all right, I understand. I deserved everything you said. It doesn't matter now, anyway. All that matters is getting you better.' She looked down anxiously at her handiwork. 'Is the bandage too tight?'

Max managed to shake his head. 'Perhaps you know what you're doing after all,' he muttered.

He seemed to lapse back into drowsiness after that. Cairo finished tying on the splint and then sat back, pushing her hair tiredly behind her ears. He was still sweating profusely and in obvious pain, but she didn't think there was much more she could do for him at the moment.

Desperate to keep herself busy, she turned her attention to sorting through Max's pack to see what supplies they had. Water wasn't an immediate problem, but she didn't know how long it would last if they had to stay there any length of time. She would have to be careful with it.

Max carried the tiny paraffin stove in his pack as well, and, after some fiddling, she managed to make it work so that she could make him some sweet tea. It seemed to revive him a little, and when he had finished she had some herself. She hadn't had anything before she set out on this morning's fateful walk, and hunger and exhaustion were combining to make her feel faint. She wouldn't be any good to Max if she passed out as well, so she ate an orange and a couple of dry biscuits.

It was the longest day of Cairo's life. About four o'clock, when the savage midday heat had lessened, she struggled back to fetch her own rucksack. It was far lighter than Max's had been, but, even so, it took all her reserves of strength to carry it to the gorge. The walk jarred every nerve in her injured ankle, but she just gritted her teeth and told herself that she deserved every moment of pain. She felt burdened down by guilt and remorse and fear.

Max hardly seemed aware that she had gone. When she put her hand on his forehead, he was burning with fever, and the glow of the setting sun deepened the flush in his cheeks.

It was the most beautiful sunset. Cairo watched the shadows lengthen and darken until every ripple in the sand, every texture in the rock was etched in black and red. She found herself noticing tiny details—the perfect curve of each pile of sand blown against the sides of the gorge, the grains glittering like metal, the shadow thrown by the battered enamel mug as it stood on the ground—

as if by concentrating on them she could forget about the nagging ache of fear for Max.

As the darkness closed in, she built a fire for comfort, using the acacia branches she had found. She had some trouble getting it started, until she remembered her Filofax. It seemed so long since she had made such a fuss about bringing it with her, and she held it between her hands, staring down at it as if it were already part of a past life. Had it really been so important to her? She remembered bitterly all those years when she had been so spoilt and indulged. She had had nothing to do with her day except enjoy herself. Couldn't she at least have done something useful, like a first-aid course? It wouldn't have taken much of her time, but at least she wouldn't have been quite so inadequate now.

She flicked through the pages of telephone numbers, recognising the names, but as if they were people she had met in some film. How many of them would be any use or comfort now? Fair-weather friends, she thought sadly, remembering how few of them had stood by her when she needed them. Piers had been a good friend, but she knew he would be as lost as she was in a situation like this. Max would never let things overwhelm him, she realised, but then Max didn't need a telephone to organise his life. Slowly, she tore out several pages and screwed them into spills.

'What are you doing?' Max whispered through cracked lips, and her stomach lurched with relief at the lucid expression in his eyes.

'Making a fire,' she told him, touching a match to one of the spills and watching the flame flicker and then burn high as it caught hold. 'I thought I would heat up some soup. You should try and have something.'

'Isn't that your precious diary you're tearing up?' His voice was weak and thready, but there was still a touch of the old acid Max in it. 'I thought you couldn't function without it?'

Cairo added a few more spills to the fire and slanted a smile at him. 'I can't. Look how useful it is now.' She assumed a virtuous expression. 'I *knew* it would come in handy.'

'And there was I thinking you didn't know what you were doing in the desert!' Max said feebly, and managed a smile.

He seemed so much better that her spirits soared, but, although he drank half a mug of soup, he soon slipped back into a restless fever which threatened to burn him up. Cairo wouldn't let herself sleep. She crouched by his side all night, holding his good hand between both of hers while he tossed and mumbled. Sometimes he called her name as if he was looking for her, and she felt her heart twist with guilt. It was all her fault.

'I'm here,' she said, the tears running down her face. 'I'm here. I won't go away. I'll do anything you say if you'll just get better, Max. Please. *Please.*'

By dawn, she was almost incoherent with exhaustion herself. She had kept the fire going all night, and was stoking it up to make some more tea when Max croaked her name behind her.

'Cairo?'

Cairo spun round. She was grimy with dust and ashes and there were huge black circles under her green eyes, but her face lit up as she saw that his fever had broken. 'Max!' she exclaimed in delight. Kneeling down beside him, she examined his face. He was looking ravaged, but his eyes were clear and the terrifying flush had died from his cheeks. 'How are you feeling?'

'I'm fine—thanks to you.' Max reached out and touched her hand very lightly. 'Who'd have thought you'd make such a good nurse?'

'I was useless,' she said bleakly, thinking of how helpless she had been to stop the onslaught of the fever.

'You weren't useless,' said Max. His eyes held a sudden glint of humour. 'You know I'd be the first person to tell you if you had been, but for once you weren't! I don't remember much about last night, but whenever I surfaced, you were always there, mopping me down, talking to me, giving me drinks of water.' He paused, and his hand tightened over hers. 'I needed you to cling on to, Cairo. Perhaps the fever would have run its course anyway, but it would have been a lot worse without you.'

The release from tension let exhaustion wash over Cairo, crashing through the barriers of her fragile self-control. Her face twisted. 'It wouldn't have happened at all without me,' she cried, and somehow her head was on his chest as she burst into tears. 'Oh, Max, I'm so sorry!' she sobbed exhaustedly. 'It was all my fault. Everything's my fault. I'm so sorry.' She knew that the last thing he needed was a hysterical woman weeping all over him, but she couldn't help herself.

Max stroked her hair with his good hand. 'It's all right,' he soothed. 'It's over now. You're exhausted, Cairo. Did you get any sleep at all?'

'I couldn't,' Cairo wept, muffled against his chest. Her shoulders heaved. 'I thought...I thought...' She couldn't finish, couldn't stop crying.

He let her cry for a bit, and then made her sit up, knuckling her eyes like a child. 'I'm sorry,' she gulped between jerky little sobs. 'I'm behaving very badly.'

Max tucked a strand of hair behind her ear with a wry smile. 'Why don't you make some tea?' he suggested patiently. 'Then you can have a sleep.'

'I couldn't sleep!' Cairo was still on the verge of hysteria. 'What about you?'

'I'm not going anywhere,' he pointed out. 'I'll be all right.' He didn't look all right to Cairo. His face was drawn with pain and he was still very weak. 'You can lie down next to me and then we can *both* sleep,' he said.

'But——'

'No arguing,' he interrupted her, and, in spite of his weakness, the teasing note was unmistakable. 'I might have been hallucinating, of course, but some time last night I could swear I heard you promise you'd do exactly as I said in the future!'

Cairo flushed. 'I did, and I will, but——'

'But nothing,' said Max, sounding more and more like himself. 'You'll be no good as a nurse if you're too tired to think straight, and, anyway, you need to rest that ankle of yours.' He frowned as he saw how swollen it was. 'You shouldn't have been carrying those packs with your leg in that condition!'

'I had to,' said Cairo, touching the ankle gingerly. She had been too worried about Max to think about it last night, but now she could feel its dull, angry ache once more.

'I know you did,' said Max more gently. He hesitated. 'I didn't think you had it in you, Cairo. I thought you were a spoilt brat who'd fall to pieces at the first sign of a crisis, but I was wrong. You may be infuriating most of the time, but last night I was glad you were here.' It was a rather backhanded compliment, but Cairo felt a glow of warmth at his approval and was suddenly, stupidly shy. 'I'll make the tea,' she muttered, unable to meet his eye.

They shared the mug of tea in silence. Max had closed his eyes as if the effort of talking had exhausted him, but he opened them as he drained the mug. 'You look terrible,' he said.

'Thanks!'

'Why don't you clean your face? You'd feel better, and since you insisted on lumping all those lotions and potions along with you you might as well use them!'

Cairo touched her face, grimacing at the sandpapery feel of her skin. 'Are you sure you can bear to watch?' she said, remembering his caustic comments last time. How long ago that seemed!

'I'll survive,' Max said. That disquieting glint of amusement was back in his eyes again. 'You've been through enough trauma without having to cope with the possibility of a wrinkle as well.'

Cairo was horrified when she examined her grimy, tear-stained face in the little mirror, and she had to use the cleanser several times before she had finally removed the last of the grime. It was extraordinarily comforting to do something as ordinary as clean her face. Max had been right. She felt ten times better already. Smoothing on moisturiser, she glanced over the top of the mirror to tell him so, only to find him watching her with a curiously arrested expression, and for some reason, she felt herself blush.

She snapped the mirror shut. 'Do I look any better?' she asked, for something to say.

'Yes.' Max's light eyes still rested on her face. 'In fact, you look the best I've ever seen you.'

Taking it as a joke, Cairo dropped the bag back into her rucksack and went to lie rather awkwardly on the sleeping mat beside him. 'I didn't realise I looked quite that bad at the camp,' she laughed, remembering wistfully how cool and clean and soft she had been then.

'You looked all right,' said Max gruffly, settling his splinted arm into a more comfortable position. He glanced at Cairo. She was looking thin, and the high, distinctive cheekbones stood out. The flawless skin was burnt brown, making her eyes look ever greener, but her features were blurred with exhaustion and her eyelids were already drooping. 'I think I prefer you like this, though,' he said quietly, so quietly that Cairo wasn't sure that she was meant to hear.

She slept all day. When she finally woke, she was lying with her face pressed against Max's shoulder, but she didn't move away immediately. It was cool and comfortable lying there in the shade, listening to his steady breathing, and in the end it was only hunger that made her stir.

There was a packet of dehydrated stew in Max's pack. The fire had long died down to a circle of white ashes, so she heated the meal on the paraffin stove, and they shared it companionably. It was as if all the tension and animosity between them had burnt out with Max's fever. Cairo felt completely different. They leant back against the rock together and watched the stars appear in the blue-black sky.

'Where did you get that damn-fool name from?' Max asked suddenly. 'Even at that wretched New Year's Eve party I can remember thinking that it was typical of you not to have an ordinary name like everyone else.'

Cairo winced at the memory of the party. It reminded her too much of the spoilt, silly girl she had been. 'I was born in Cairo,' she said. 'I don't remember it at all, but my father always said that they were so happy there they decided to call me after the city.' She gave a reminiscent smile, thinking of her father. 'He was always very romantic.'

'Romantic? Jeremy Kingswood? You are his daughter, aren't you?'

She nodded, wondering if Max knew about the scandal surrounding her father, but his next words seemed to indicate that the news hadn't yet reached the Sahara.

'I wouldn't have guessed he was romantic,' he said with an ironic look. 'I always thought he was one of the most successful businessmen around—and the most ruthless.'

Cairo was silent. Many people had thought that of her father, and most had rejoiced at his downfall. 'He wasn't ever like that with me,' she said at last. 'My mother died when I was very small, so we were always close. He used to spoil me. I think a lot of people thought he would buy me presents to stop him feeling guilty about not being around all the time, but it wasn't like that at all. I just loved being with him.'

She paused to watch a shooting star drop into the blackness. Until she came to the desert and met Max, she had never realised quite how spoilt she had been. She had taken her father's love for granted, she realised. The luxury she had grown up in had made her just as vain and self-centred as Max had said, and she remembered uncomfortably how she had behaved with Max at the beginning. No wonder he hadn't liked her.

'It wasn't the presents that spoilt me, though,' she went on slowly. 'It was growing up knowing that for my father I was special, adored no matter what I did.' Cairo gave a rueful smile. Max would never think of her like that. 'I suppose I got too used to having my own way. My father never criticised me. I used to think he was perfect.'

Max looked at her curiously. 'Used to?' he echoed. 'Don't you think he's perfect any more?'

Cairo thought of the revelations that had come out in the newspapers when the Company Fraud Office had first been called in to investigate her father's affairs. She had learnt then of a man who seemed to have no connection with her adoring father.

'No, I don't think he's perfect,' she said quietly. 'But I still love him. He's my father. Nothing can change that.' Forgetting that Max was unaware of the scandal surrounding her father, she sent him a challenging look, half expecting him to scoff, but the eyes that met hers held an unreadable expression.

'You're more forgiving than I am,' he said, looking away. His voice was bitter. 'I thought my mother was perfect until I was nine, but as far as I was concerned she stopped being my mother when she left Joanna and me behind. Joanna's four years younger than I am. You can imagine what it does to a little girl of five to be abandoned by her mother.'

Cairo said nothing. She could also imagine what it had been like for a small boy of nine, who had thought his mother was perfect.

'Our father didn't want anything to remind him of our mother, so we were left to our own devices a lot,' Max went on after a moment. 'I always felt responsible for Joanna.' He shrugged. 'I suppose I still do. She's always been so vulnerable. Because she was so young when our mother left, she used to glamourise her, and then tried to imitate her when she was older. She let herself be swept into that social world, but she just can't cope with all the hypocrisy and double dealings.' He sighed, and Cairo was conscious of a pang of jealousy that *she* couldn't provoke that look of concern on his face. 'Whenever things go wrong for Joanna, I have to go back to London and sort her out.'

'Can't she sort herself out?' Cairo asked, more tartly than she intended. 'I thought she was supposed to be like me?'

'Only superficially. Joanna's not strong like you.'

'I wasn't strong until I had to be,' said Cairo, thinking of how quickly she had had to learn to cope when her father's world collapsed.

'Perhaps, but I don't think Joanna would ever have been able to cope with a crisis the way you did. She's always been so unsure of herself. Joanna does have charm, but she's a pastel person, whereas you...' He broke off, and his eyes rested on Cairo's face. 'You're more vivid.'

Cairo's eyes met his with a jolt that caught the breath in her throat, and there was a moment of taut silence before he turned away, as if regretting his words. 'Joanna needs someone to look after her,' he continued, and Cairo felt disappointment settle coldly around her. She had been so sure that he was warming to her, but it seemed he was far more concerned with his sister.

His face had darkened. 'That ought to have been her husband's job. I never liked him—he was a typical advertising executive—but Joanna would marry him. It was obvious he was only interested in her money, and now that he's spent most of it he's decided to dump her in favour of some eighteen-year-old model. Joanna was devastated, but just as she seems to be getting over Toby she's gone and got herself involved with someone who sounds just as unsuitable. The same type of smooth operator, full of pseudo-charm and practised lies. Not only that, she thinks he's already having an affair with another woman.' Max rubbed the bridge of his nose in a worried gesture. 'Joanna's letters are getting more and more fraught. If it goes on like this, I'll have to go back to London and see her.'

Cairo couldn't help thinking that Joanna might cope better if she didn't have her capable elder brother to rely on. Max obviously adored his sister, she thought with another pinch of jealousy. She wished she hadn't coped so well now. Perhaps if she had been more pathetic, Max would realise that *she* needed someone to look after her as well.

She wondered if he would go to London as he had said. Cairo found it hard to imagine him in the city, wearing a suit and striding along the crowded streets. She couldn't imagine him anywhere but here, in his battered hat and shabby, oil-stained clothes, completely at home under the vast desert sky.

If he *did* come to London, she would be able to see him again. The thought slid insidiously into Cairo's mind with a small thrill of expectation, followed immediately by the cruel realisation that Max might not want to see her. Why should he? He had been so much nicer since she had nursed him through his fever, but it didn't mean he had changed his mind about her. She would still represent everything he most despised about his mother's lifestyle. She had behaved like the spoilt, arrogant brat he had accused her of being, and in the end she had even put his life at risk. Why on earth would he want to see her after she had made such a thorough nuisance of herself? Max had every reason to dislike her, Cairo realised dismally, and would probably breathe a sigh of relief when he finally got rid of her.

CHAPTER SIX

TWISTING the enamel mug round in her hands, Cairo glanced at Max under her lashes. He was looking up at the stars, his eyes narrowed in thought, and as her gaze drifted over the planes of his face, over the angular cheekbones, along the stubborn line of his jaw, to rest inevitably on his mouth, she felt a slow trembling start deep inside.

It was just reaction, she told herself in panic. Anyone would feel strange after a sleepless night. She didn't really want to reach over and touch him, to make him turn and smile and kiss her and say that of course he wanted to see her again. Of course she didn't. She was simply suffering from a classic patient-nurse syndrome. She had been worrying about him so much over the last few hours that now she was obsessed with him, that was all.

Without warning, Max turned his head to find her watching him, and their eyes locked before she had a chance to look away. Cairo felt as if a hand was squeezing tight around her heart. She couldn't move, couldn't breathe. All she could do was look helplessly into Max's eyes, dark and indecipherable in the moonlight, and wonder if he could read the longing written in her own.

You're not in love with him, she told herself as she lay next to him that night, trying not to think about how close he was. You've got nothing in common. He belongs in the desert, you belong in the city. He's cool and self-contained, you're frivolous and spoilt. He's simply not your type. Falling for someone who despised you was just asking for trouble.

I can't be in love with him, she decided. I won't be.

*   *   *

'Our water's not going to last much longer,' Cairo said to Max the next morning. She was being studiously brisk and practical, and was making a point of keeping a careful distance from him.

She doubted if Max even noticed. He lay on his sleeping mat, drawn and rather listless. He had slept restlessly, and she knew he was still in pain, though he refused to admit it.

He pulled one of the empty water containers towards him now, grimacing as the movement jarred his arm, and shook it with a frown. 'I'd better go and get some more,' he said. 'There's a guelta a couple of hours from here where the water table comes to the surface. I could fill up there.'

'You can't walk for a couple of hours,' Cairo protested, horrified. 'I'll go.'

'With your ankle?' Max struggled to sit up. 'You'd never make it.'

'*I* haven't had a raging fever,' she pointed out tartly. 'And my ankle's much better. Look.' She tested it on the ground to show him, although it took a heroic effort not to wince.

Max was hauling himself to his feet, putting his hand out against the rock to steady himself. 'You can't possibly go on your own,' he said, irritated by his own weakness. 'You'd get lost.'

'You could draw me a map.'

'No,' he said as they faced each other stubbornly. 'I'm not letting you go.'

If only he meant it, Cairo thought wistfully, and then pulled herself up. She wasn't in love with him, she'd decided that last night. No matter what happened, she would have to go back to London in the end, and she didn't want to think about how desolate she was going to feel then.

'Max, you're not strong enough to go,' she told him firmly. 'Look at you, you can hardly stand!'

'I'm all right,' he said obstinately.

'You're *not* all right! You're sick!'

'Don't nag, woman!' snapped Max, exasperated. 'If you're going to make such a fuss, we'll both go.'

It took them much longer than two hours, and the walk was a struggle for both of them, but neither would admit it, and they kept each other going until they arrived at last at the guelta.

There, where the water table ran near the surface, oleanders flourished in a riot of pink flowers, their narrow grey-green leaves silver-bright in the sun. The pool itself was still and secretive, edged with rushes and lilies, and a lizard with a bright blue back lay sleepily sunning himself on a rock.

An air of peace and profusion hung over the tiny oasis. Cairo forgot the jabbing pain in her ankle as she limped beside Max below a line of cedar trees humming with bees. They shared an orange at the water's edge, and she felt a sensuous lethargy steal over her. The orange juice was sweet on her tongue, sticky where it dribbled down her chin, and the faint fragrance of the oleanders drifted on the hot, dry air.

Max sat beside her, listening to the bees. Everything about him seemed very distinct. Cairo could see the dust on his hat and the lines of exhaustion at either side of his mouth. The walk had been a nightmare for him, but he had refused to give in, and it was only by pretending that her ankle hurt that she had persuaded him to stop frequently and rest.

The water from the guelta looked green and unappetising, but Max rigged up a filter, and then they boiled it before pouring it into their containers and dropping in sterilising tablets for good measure. They talked easily together as they worked, and, when they had finished, sat by the guelta and shared a mug of tea. Cairo had always been a girl who liked champagne and cocktails, but sitting on a boulder next to Max, with the air sweet and vibrant with bees, passing the enamel mug between them, she knew that no drink would ever taste better than that tea.

'It's beautiful here, isn't it?' she sighed, her eyes on the cedar trees and the stark grandeur of the gorge beyond.

Max glanced at her. 'I never thought I'd hear you say that the desert was beautiful. I thought you hated it?'

'I did,' said Cairo, wondering just when she had changed her mind. 'I suppose I just got used to it,' she added lamely. 'I still find it all a bit overwhelming, but it doesn't terrify me the way it did before.'

'Perhaps you'll have got something out of this trip after all,' said Max. 'You've had to learn a lot about yourself over the last few days. It's probably not what you wanted to take back with you from the plateau, but self-knowledge is a far more useful thing than finding a few locations for some ridiculous commercial.'

'I suppose so,' said Cairo glumly. Max's words had brought back all the problems she had pushed to the back of her mind. What was she going to do about arranging a shoot for Haydn Deane? They would be expecting to hear from her any day now.

Max seemed to read her mind. 'At least you tried. It's not your fault that some idiotic executive chose somewhere totally inaccessible for the shoot.'

'No,' Cairo sighed. 'You were right all along. It was a stupid idea.' She looked around her, at the still, silent magnificence of the scenery. 'Even if it *were* possible, I don't know that I'd want to bring a team of fashion people up here, all giggling and gossiping and complaining,' she said slowly. 'It would spoil everything.' She glanced at Max. 'I can understand now why you didn't want to bring me with you. I'm sorry. I shouldn't have forced myself on you like that. You must have thought I was just as bad.'

Amusement touched the corners of Max's mouth. 'Actually, I thought you were worse.'

'*Worse*?' Surely she hadn't been *that* bad? Cairo's lips tightened in chagrin, but when she stole another glance at him she saw that he was smiling.

'I've changed my mind,' he assured her. His voice was deep and very warm, and Cairo's heart leapt. Careful, she reminded herself.

'You mean I'm only "just as bad"?' she said, determined not to be caught out twice.

'No,' said Max. 'You're better.' There was a pause. 'Much better,' he added softly.

Cairo didn't dare look at him. She could feel a tide of heat surging up her throat and spreading over her cheeks. She cleared her throat.

'Er—I...good...good...' Heavens, she was stammering like a schoolgirl! 'I'll tell the advertisers that a shoot on the plateau really isn't practical,' she said, desperately forcing herself back to normality. Her voice sounded horribly squeaky, and she cleared her throat again. 'It just doesn't look very good for our business if our first job turns out to be an abject failure.'

'Suggest somewhere else,' said Max. He must have noticed her confusion, but gave no sign of it.

'Where?' Cairo's voice had returned to normal and she was worrying in earnest now. 'I haven't got time to scour the desert for another location and make all the arrangements.'

'Why can't you just go back and tell them the truth? That the desert's no place for them. They could make just as effective an advertisement in a London studio!'

'I know,' said Cairo. 'But if I say that, they won't offer us any more jobs and they won't recommend us to anyone either. They'll just think I wasn't capable of making the arrangements.'

Piers would think that too. Cairo's green eyes shadowed as she remembered how much depended on her making a success of this job. Her father's haggard face swam into her mind.

'I've got to go back with *something*,' she said, determinedly.

'Is this job really so important to you?'

Cairo thought about the promise she had made her father. She thought about her godmother who had had enough faith in her to lend her the capital to start up the business, and about Piers who had swept her along on the tide of his enthusiasm. The job wasn't important, but they were. She didn't want to go back to London to battle with her father's debts. She wanted to sit on and on with Max in this tranquil oasis and never have to leave, but she couldn't let them down.

'Yes,' she said quietly. 'It is.'

Max's eyes rested on her face. 'I could take you to a couple of sites when we get back to the camp if you like,' he offered abruptly. 'They'd make a spectacular backdrop to any photographs, and you'd be able to reach them by four-wheel-drive from Menesset without any problems.'

'Could you?' Cairo's face lit up, and then her smile faded in puzzlement. 'Why would you do that for me after all the trouble I've been?'

There was a pause. 'I know what lengths you'll go to to get this wretched job done,' Max said gruffly after a moment. 'I dread to think what would happen if you decide to go jaunting about the desert by yourself. At least if I go with you, I don't need to be wondering just what kind of trouble you've got yourself into. Besides, I've got to collect some samples from that area. I could do that at the same time.'

Cairo glowed at the thought. She would still have to leave, she reminded herself hastily, and this tingling warmth was just relief at the prospect of finding a possible site for Haydn Deane. It had absolutely nothing to do with the fact that she could spend an extra day or two with Max.

'Thank you,' she said simply, and, without thinking, she reached over and touched his hand. 'I'll do whatever you tell me,' she promised.

'I'll believe that when I see it,' Max grunted, but his mouth twitched, and when his eyes met Cairo's neither could resist smiling. His teeth looked very white against his tanned face and the light eyes were warmer than she had ever seen them.

Careful, Cairo told herself as her heart soared. It's only a smile. So what if his eyes crease with secret laughter and just looking at his mouth makes it hard to breathe? It doesn't mean you're in love with him. It just means you've been alone together for too long.

His grin was fading, but his eyes held hers. Cairo could feel the air tighten between them, and she took her hand uncertainly from his. The bees humming in the background seemed unnaturally loud. He's going to kiss me, she thought with a queer mixture of panic and exhilaration, and she knew that she would never be able to control her reactions if he did.

'I...I...' She swallowed. 'What about some more tea?'

Max's eyes shuttered. 'Good idea,' he said.

Two days later, they were climbing down towards the pick-up truck which was waiting for Max in the shade. Far below them, it looked like a model car left by some child in a giant sandpit. Cairo watched it with mixed feelings. Part of her longed to have finished this gruelling walk, and part wanted to stop time so that she could stay on the plateau alone with Max. Reaching that truck would be like stepping back to reality.

He had promised to show her some different locations. Cairo found herself clinging to the prospect. At least it meant that she didn't have to say goodbye as soon as they reached the foot of the plateau.

The last two and a half days had been difficult. Since that moment at the guelta, Max seemed to have withdrawn. The rather wary warmth they had established together had dissolved into a new and more unsettling tension. One minute they would be talking quite easily together, the next their eyes would meet and conversation would falter while the atmosphere between them tightened yet another screw.

Lying stiffly next to Max at night, Cairo would wonder whether it would have been different if she hadn't jumped up to make the tea. Would Max have kissed her? Would his lips have been cool and persuasive against hers, and how would he have reacted to the aching need of her response? Cairo told herself she was glad she hadn't allowed herself the chance to find out.

It was impossible to know what Max was thinking. Sometimes she would look up to find him watching her, but his guarded expression gave nothing away. He might never have intended to kiss her at all. His arm was still bandaged, but he had recovered remarkably quickly from the fever, and sometimes she wondered dismally if his illness had been the only reason for the unexpected understanding that had flowered so briefly between them.

It's better this way, Cairo reminded herself as she rounded another sharp twist in the path. Her ankle was much improved, except for the occasional twinge, but going down was proving to be even worse than climbing up the plateau. The weight of her pack threatened to tip her forwards, and her knees trembled with the effort of keeping her balance.

Max was even more remote and withdrawn today. Cairo worried that he might be still suffering the after-effects of the venom, but he brushed her concern aside.

'I thought you were in a hurry to get home?' he said when she suggested resting at the camp for a day before starting the long trek down.

Cairo thought of Haydn Deane drumming their fingers on their glossy desks as they waited for her to report back to them. 'I am, but it's not worth you collapsing halfway down.'

'I'm not going to collapse,' Max said irritably. 'The sooner we get off this plateau, the better.'

Did that mean he was anxious to get rid of her? Cairo wondered miserably.

The things Max had made her leave behind were still sitting behind the boulder with the white stone on top of them. It was hard to believe that she could ever have thought that she would need them. They all seemed quite irrelevant now, Cairo thought as she packed them slowly away in her rucksack.

After one surprised look, the driver seemed to take Cairo's presence for granted, and he chatted cheerfully to Max in Arabic as they jolted over the corrugations, evidently exclaiming over the story of the snakebite. Cairo wondered if Max was telling him that it had all been her fault. She was squeezed between the two men on the bench seat, and stared out of the window, trying not to think about the lean strength of Max's thigh pressed against hers, or the arm which he was resting along the back of the seat. If she tipped her head back, she could lean against it.

She might have been a rather awkwardly shaped rucksack for all the notice Max took of her. He talked to the driver the whole way while she sat silently between them with a brittle look of unconcern on her face.

When they got to the camp, Cairo climbed out and stood uncertainly by the truck. It felt strange to be surrounded by buildings and people again. Everything seemed small and unimpressive after the towering gorges on the plateau.

'I presume you left your things with Bruce?' Max said, lifting her rucksack out of the back of the truck and dropping it on the ground beside her in a cloud of dust.

Cairo nodded. 'He said I could use the guest room as long as I wanted.'

'I'll bet he did,' said Max nastily. 'You've got a night here, so I'm sure he'll be only too delighted to catch up with you again. If you want to go and see these sites, we'll have to leave at five o'clock tomorrow morning. I'm sure you're desperate to get back to civilisation.'

'Yes,' she said flatly. This was the old, hostile Max. Nothing had changed. How had she ever thought that it could? Making him a few cups of tea while he had a fever wasn't going to convince him that she was anything other than a thoughtless, superficial city girl like his mother.

Cairo looked down at her rucksack, remembering what he had said about her learning something from her experience on the plateau. He had said that she had coped, that she had guts. Once or twice, he had almost seemed to like her. It was as if coming back to the camp had reminded him of all the things she represented, and that he hated so much.

She wanted to shout at him, to tell him that she *had* changed, that she wasn't quite the same girl who had demanded to be taken up the plateau. Max had done more for her than simply guide her through the rocks, and it suddenly seemed very important to tell him that.

'Max, I . . .' she began, and then stopped, unsure of how to thank him properly.

He looked at her, his light eyes suddenly alert. 'Yes?'

'I just——'

'Cairo!' Bruce had caught sight of them as he was driving past, and he brought the car to a stop with a squeal of brakes and jumped out. 'What a wonderful surprise!' Before Cairo had a chance to say all she wanted to Max, he was bearing down on them, a delighted smile on his face.

'You're a sight for sore eyes,' he said. 'Only a girl like you could spend several days on the plateau and still look as beautiful as when she set out!'

Cairo had found Bruce charming before; now his compliments seemed empty and ridiculous, but he had been more than generous in giving her the use of a room and his car, and she could hardly snub him.

'Hello, Bruce.' She smiled and let him catch hold of her hands and kiss her on both cheeks. Over his shoulder, she could see Max looking boot-faced. He obviously thought she was being superficial again. What did he expect her to do? she thought in a sudden burst of anger. Push Bruce away?

Bruce was picking up her rucksack, insisting on driving her along to the guest rooms. Cairo felt stifled by his effusive personality. Max would have made her carry her own pack and walk.

He was watching Bruce fussing round her with a saturnine expression. Cairo glanced at him, hoping against hope that he would suggest meeting her later, but he merely gave her a curt nod.

'I'll see you tomorrow morning. Don't be late,' he said, and walked off without another word.

Was that all he could say, after all they had been through together? Cairo was hurt and angry, and too proud to show it. Instead, she turned to Bruce with a brilliant smile and let him bear her off to her room.

She was horrified when she caught sight of herself in the mirror. Her face was sunburnt and so thickly covered in dust and sand that she hardly recognised herself. She looked tired and thin, and her hair felt like straw. Only the blazing green eyes were the same.

'I prefer you this way'. She could remember the timbre of Max's voice, the exquisite relief of knowing that she could sleep, knowing that he was there beside her. The shade had been deep and cool, and when she had woken her face had been pressed against his upper arm so that she could breathe in the smell of his skin . . .

Cairo shook herself free of the memories, horrified at the look of dark, naked longing in the eyes that stared back at her from the mirror. She mustn't do this to herself. She must think about finding a location for Haydn Deane, about going home, about seeing her father and telling him she had made a start at paying off his debts, about anything other than Max and the way he walked and the way he turned his head and the way his hands felt against her skin.

She felt better after a shower. She had to wash her hair three times to get out all the sand and tangles, but at last it bounced silkily about her jawline in thick, streaky golden waves. Her face was still very brown, but at least it was clean, and her slanting eyes shone a deep, clear green.

Cairo slipped on a cool, silky blue dress and felt more like her old self. Bruce was openly admiring when he picked her up and walked her over to the mess, but although she tried hard to respond she couldn't help missing Max's astringency. This was ridiculous! She had only been away from him for two hours, and already her pulse had quickened at the thought of seeing him again.

He wasn't there.

The disappointment was so sharp that Cairo wanted to cry. She had never cried over a man, she reminded herself fiercely. Never! Bruce didn't seem to notice anything amiss, so she supposed she must have talked and smiled automatically, but later she had no idea what had been said. All she could think about was that Max didn't even care enough to come along and have a drink with her.

If he had walked into the bar then, she would have thrown herself into his arms, but the realisation made Cairo so angry with herself that she pulled herself together sharply. She was being utterly pathetic! What had she allowed to happen to herself if *she*, Cairo Kingswood, had let herself get into this kind of state about some grumpy geologist? He was more interested in his precious rocks than he was in her!

She wasn't going to waste any more time thinking about him. Her chin lifted in unconscious pride. If she hadn't known that he was her best chance of finding a location in such a short time, she would have told him that she never wanted to see him again. As it was, she

owed it to Piers and Haydn Deane at least to go, but
this time it would be on strictly businesslike terms. She
would take some photographs, arrange guides and
permits in Menesset and go home. Cairo told herself she
couldn't wait.

She pretended not to notice Max when he finally appeared, even though her heart gave a great lurch at the
sight of his cool, austere figure in the door of the mess.
His eyes flickered towards her, but he didn't even smile.
He just went calmly up to the counter, helped himself
to a meal and went over to sit on the other side of the
room.

Cairo sucked in her breath through clenched teeth.
She had practically crippled herself carrying his rucksack
along the gorge to give him some water, she had worried
herself sick about him, she had even torn up her Filofax
to make him tea, and he couldn't even be bothered to
come over and say hello!

Her green eyes glittered dangerously. Turning deliberately to Bruce, she gave him a dazzling smile that made
him blink, and spent the rest of the evening showing
Max, if he had cared to look, just what a charming,
seductive, witty woman he was ignoring.

Bruce clearly couldn't believe his luck. Cairo risked
an occasional glance beneath her lashes at Max to see
how he was reacting, but, to her fury, he merely looked
dour and quite uninterested. He ate his meal, exchanged
a few words with the other men at his table, and walked
out, leaving Cairo feeling curiously deflated.

She slept fitfully that night, unaccustomed to the soft
bed. It was hard to imagine how scared she had been
the first night she had slept out under the stars. Now
the walls and ceiling confined her, and the rattle of the
air-conditioner grated on her nerves. She missed Max
more than she was prepared to admit. Somehow she had
got used to listening to him breathing and knowing that
she only had to reach out to touch his reassuring strength.

The restless night left her tired and irritable, and Max was clearly feeling much the same when she hurried up to him the next morning. It was twenty past five.

Cairo had been unable to face the prospect of putting on her grubby shorts again, and had pulled a dress out of her suitcase. It was a cool, comfortable cotton in soft pinks and greens, buttoning down the front of her waist and then hanging in soft folds around her slender legs. It would be ideal for sitting in a car all day, she had thought as she pulled it hurriedly out of her suitcase at five o'clock. After tossing and turning all night, she had dropped into a deep sleep in the early hours and had overslept. Max would be unimpressed—if he was still there.

He was there, but the sardonic expression on his face told her that she had guessed correctly.

'Where do you think you're going?' he demanded. 'A garden party?'

Cairo's lips tightened. She had hoped to overwhelm Max with her cool femininity, but he showed no signs of being overwhelmed. She was determined not to let him guess how long she had spent thinking about him, and tattered pride was making her tense and defensive. 'What's wrong with my dress?' she demanded. 'We're going in a vehicle, aren't we?'

'We are,' Max confirmed. He nodded his head at a battered old jeep standing near by. 'That's it over there.'

Cairo stared at it, appalled. 'I thought we'd be going in the pick-up.'

'The pick-up isn't mine. I just get a lift in it occasionally. The rest of the time I use the jeep.'

'But there's no roof!' she wailed. 'I'll get filthy again!'

'It'll just be a bit of sand. You have to expect that in the desert,' said Max with a predictable lack of sympathy.

'I'm going back to put on my shorts,' said Cairo, turning, but was brought up by a hard hand on her arm.

'Oh, no, you don't. You're already twenty minutes late, and I'm not waiting any longer.'

'But my dress is going to get ruined!'

'Tough,' said Max. 'If you didn't learn about wearing sensible clothes when we went up the plateau, that's your problem.' He picked up Cairo's pack and tossed it in the back of the jeep. 'Get in.'

Sulking, Cairo wrestled with the door, opened it with difficulty and brushed fastidiously at the dusty seat before she sat down.

'I don't know why you bother with doors if you haven't got a roof,' she grumbled.

'Stop complaining,' he said, starting the engine. 'You wanted to come, and there are no other vehicles available at this short notice. You're lucky I'm taking you at all. You're the one who's in such a tearing hurry to get back to London.'

'If we went later, would we be able to have a car with air-conditioning?' Cairo was unable to resist asking.

'You've changed your tune, haven't you?' said Max unpleasantly. 'At the guelta you were panicking about not getting home in time.'

'I do have to get back.' Cairo sighed, remembering. 'Piers will be waiting and——'

'Piers?' Max interrupted her.

She threw him a curious look. 'He's my partner,' she explained.

'Not Piers Ward-Willoughby, by any chance?' he asked in a strangely grim tone.

'Yes.' Cairo turned to look at him, astonished at the coincidence. 'Do you know him?' Where on earth would Max have come across the sociable, charming Piers? They were chalk and cheese!

'I know of him,' Max said in the same ominous voice. 'Which means I also know all about *you*.'

'Me?'

'I gather you and Piers spend a lot of time together?' he went on with heavy sarcasm.

Cairo was completely baffled. 'He's my partner. Of course I see a lot of him.'

'I don't suppose it bothers you that he's running around with two women at one time?'

'I don't suppose you could tell me what you're talking about?' Cairo retorted in a frigid voice. She was fed up with this!

Max changed gear angrily. 'Joanna's in love with Piers—or she thinks she is. Her letters are full of him. She's just got over her divorce, and this Piers is making her miserable.'

What did that have to do with *her*? Cairo wondered angrily. 'It doesn't sound like Piers,' she said curtly. He had always preferred to make his way by charm rather than hard work. He could be tiresomely flippant at times, but never cruel. 'He's not a heartless schemer, if that's what you're worried about. I can't believe he'd hurt anyone deliberately.'

'That's what Joanna says. Apparently there's another woman in the background who's got her claws into him. From all I can gather, this Piers is just after her money, but Joanna says he really loves her and it's this other woman who's determined to have him. She's afraid she's going to lose him.'

Cairo was sick of hearing about Joanna and her problems. 'It sounds to me as if your sister is being completely wet,' she said roundly. Nearly as wet as she had been about Max last night, but she was over that now, she reminded herself hastily. 'If she's so in love with Piers, why doesn't she stand up and fight for him?'

'Joanna's not a fighter like you.' Max's jaw was set as he glanced at Cairo. 'She can be pretty when she tries, but she's got no confidence in herself. She wouldn't stand much of a chance against you.'

Cairo stared at him, as the realisation struck. 'You don't really think this other woman is *me*, do you?'

'It seems fairly obvious,' said Max tightly. 'According to Joanna, Piers spends an awful lot of time with this woman, who's beautiful and glamorous and confident—all the things Joanna isn't, and you are. Not only that, she's trying to get Piers involved in some shady business scheme that Joanna thinks will ruin him.'

'Joanna doesn't know what she's talking about,' said Cairo in tight-lipped emphasis when she could speak. For a moment she had been so taken aback that she could only gape at Max, but now white hot fury was searing through her. 'Piers may well be having an affair with her, although I've never so much as heard him mention a Joanna, but he certainly isn't having an affair with *me!*'

CHAPTER SEVEN

MAX looked at her suspiciously. 'You don't deny you're in business with him?'

'No. Why should I?' Cairo shook back her hair angrily. 'But if you think that I've slogged all over that wretched plateau for a *shady* business, you and your precious Joanna have got another think coming! And for the record,' she swept on, 'I did *not* inveigle Piers into the business. It was his idea, not mine, and we're partners in the purely business sense of the word, so you can tell Joanna that, too!'

Max was silent, a muscle working furiously in his jaw, obviously unwilling to be convinced. 'I can understand why Joanna felt threatened by you,' he said after a while.

'It's more than I can,' said Cairo tartly. 'I've never even met her.'

'She must have seen you somewhere. You've got all the looks and confidence that she lacks, and enough wealth to tempt Piers. I gather he hasn't got any money, and is the sort of man on the lookout for a rich wife. He couldn't do much better than Jeremy Kingswood's daughter, could he?'

Cairo began to laugh. If only he knew! Jeremy Kingswood's daughter had nothing but debts and liabilities, as Piers well knew. She and Piers were as desperate as each other to make some money. 'I suppose you could say that it was money that brought us together,' she gasped at last.

'I'm glad you find it so amusing,' Max said coldly. 'I don't happen to find it funny that my sister is being made miserable, for whatever reason, but I'm prepared to accept that you're not having an affair with Piers if you say so.'

125

'Big of you!' said Cairo in an acid voice, and turned her face deliberately away. He was unbearable. Arrogant, pigheaded, prejudiced and absolutely insufferable! How could she ever have even *considered* being in love with him? She hated him! How dared he accuse her of having an affair with Piers just because his sister was too stupid to ask Piers outright?

Chin tilted aggressively, Cairo stared through the cracked windscreen. She wished she'd never embarked on this awful trip. She'd never been in such a dilapidated vehicle before; it was little more than a sand-encrusted chassis with tattered seats and a jumble of wires holding the whole thing together under the bare metal dash-board. It was a wonder it could go at all.

They were driving away from the plateau, and the desert was flat and featureless and monotonously brown beneath a huge, burningly blue sky. The track itself was well used, ridged with corrugations, and the jeep rattled and protested madly as they raced over them, jolting across a tyre track every now and then with spine-jarring impact.

Cairo was not enjoying herself. She had looked forward to the luxury of travelling by car rather than on foot, but she had imagined a smooth, air-conditioned vehicle, not this boneshaking old rustbucket which seemed to suck in the dust. It got everywhere, lay thick on the metal dashboard and the seat between them, stuck to her skin and her hair and coated her dress in a layer of dull brown. To add insult to injury, Max somehow managed to look as cool and clean as when they had set out.

I hate him, said Cairo to herself again.

They drove for a couple of hours before Max sud-denly veered off the piste and headed over towards a ridge in the distance. Cairo preserved an icy silence and refused to ask where they were going, but as they got closer the ridge resolved itself into a mass of black, dramatic rocks, their stark silhouettes softened by the sweep of glittering sand dunes.

Cairo got stiffly out of the car. She could see already that it would be a perfect site for the shoot, but she didn't feel like giving Max the satisfaction of telling him so. Instead, she ostentatiously ignored him and took a whole roll of film from different angles. When she looked round, Max had disappeared, presumably to survey some of his precious rocks. Much she cared! Cairo sat on a rock in the meagre shade and fanned herself with her notebook. There was no doubt that this was the ideal spot.

After a while she began to get bored and look at her watch. Max was taking his time, but she was damned if she was going to go and look for him. The sky glared down at her and the heat bounced off the rocks as the minutes ticked away, and when there was still no sign of Max she was sure that he was keeping her waiting deliberately.

'Where have you been?' she demanded when he finally strolled back into view holding some obscure surveying instrument.

'Working,' he said shortly. 'Contrary to what you seem to believe, I have other things to do than dance attendance on you. I'm doing you a big enough favour letting you come along at all without jumping to attention whenever you snap your fingers.'

'There's no need to be such a martyr about it,' snapped Cairo. 'You offered to bring me, *if* you remember. If it was going to be such a trauma for you, you should have kept your mouth shut.'

Max threw the instrument in the back of the jeep. 'Is it too much to hope that you could keep yours shut?' he said unpleasantly.

Cairo had to struggle with the door again, and relieved her feelings when she finally got in by banging it shut.

'Don't slam the door!' snarled Max.

'Why not? Afraid the whole thing will fall apart?'

'There's nothing wrong with this jeep!'

'No, nothing that a new chassis, new doors, new windscreen and a new engine wouldn't cure!'

'It works perfectly well,' said Max through gritted teeth. 'That's what's important. Of course, it's typical of you to be more concerned by how a thing looks rather than how it operates. Personally, I'd put reliability over appearance any day—and that goes for people as well as cars!'

He turned the key in the ignition as he spoke, only to produce an ominous grinding noise, followed by silence.

'Sorry, what was that about reliability?' Cairo asked, sugar sweet.

Max shot her a filthy look and tried the key again, with exactly the same result. Swearing under his breath, he groped beneath the dashboard for the bonnet-release handle.

'What's wrong?'

'The engine won't start,' he said curtly, and Cairo bridled.

'I may not be the world's best mechanic, but even I could work that one out!'

Max straightened. 'Do you know one end of a combustion engine from another?' he asked between clenched teeth.

'I know how to check the oil.'

'That'll be a big help,' he said sarcastically.

'There's no need to be so patronising,' Cairo snapped. 'I only wanted to know what was wrong. I don't want to be stuck in the desert with you again!'

'The feeling is quite mutual,' said Max in an icy voice. 'I don't happen to *know* what's wrong yet. For a start, I can't see through metal, so I don't know what's going on in the engine, and, even if I did, the answer wouldn't mean anything to you.'

'It might,' lied Cairo. 'I'm not a complete idiot.'

'Then why do you behave like one?' Max asked, provoked beyond endurance. Jumping down from the jeep, he banged his door shut with unnecessary force and strode round to the front of the vehicle.

'Don't slam the door!' she shouted after him.

Max glared at her through the windscreen, but contented himself with jerking up the bonnet and cutting her from his view.

Cairo sat, arms folded defiantly, and glowered through the cracked windscreen at the lid of the bonnet. It had been a sort of dull green once, but was now so ingrained with sand that it looked brown.

Why was Max being so obnoxious? For a dangerous moment, Cairo allowed herself to remember the man she had known on the plateau. He had stroked her hair when she had cried, and held her in his arms to keep away the terrors of the night. She could remember every time he had smiled at her, every time he had touched her. Cairo's mind veered away from remembering how he had kissed her, and she scowled at the bonnet. She hadn't ever liked him, really. She had just been dependent on him, and she wasn't going to be dependent on him much longer. He might have had his moments on the plateau, but they had been exceptions, and since they had come down he had been downright unpleasant. Well, that was fine by her, Cairo thought huffily. She would just ignore him.

She concentrated on ignoring Max for a few minutes, but when he still didn't emerge from behind the bonnet, she succumbed to curiosity and climbed down, after another short, sharp altercation with the door, and went to peer over his shoulder at the engine.

'Well?'

He glanced at her with dislike. 'If it means anything to you, the carburettor has seized up.'

'Oh.' Cairo tried to look as if she knew what a carburettor was. 'Will you be able to fix it?'

'Probably. I'll have to strip the carburettor right down, though.'

'Can I do anything?'

Max sighed irritably. 'The most useful thing you can do is sit down and shut up. I can't concentrate with you hanging over me like that.'

'I was only trying to help,' said Cairo, affronted.

'Well, help by keeping out of my way and not asking any more stupid questions!'

Offended, Cairo turned on her heel and went back to her seat. Let him do it all by himself, then! She had left the door open this time to save her nails and her temper any further wear, but still her resentment simmered as she swung her legs up on to the bench seat and settled herself as comfortably as she could. It looked like being a long, hot wait.

The minutes crawled by in oppressive heat, the silence broken only by the sound of Max tinkering away at the engine and a solitary fly which had appeared out of nowhere and was buzzing around Cairo's face. What was it doing out *here*? Cairo wondered irritably, flicking it away with her notebook. There was nothing here for a fly or anything else. Only rocks and sky and sand.

The fly landed on her arm and she slapped at it. Why didn't it go and buzz around Max? Cairo was thoroughly hot and bored by the time she remembered a magazine she had stuffed into her rucksack at the last minute. She hadn't had time to read it on the plane, and she had brought it along in case she needed a good excuse to ignore Max.

Clambering over into the back, she rummaged around in her pack and pulled the magazine out triumphantly. At least she could read to take her mind off the sweat trickling down her back and how horrible Max was being.

The magazine looked glossy and somehow out of place in the dusty jeep. Cairo weighed it in her hands and then, on an impulse, lifted it to her face so that she could smell the paper, overcome by a wave of nostalgia for people, places, civilisation, anything other than this vast, brown emptiness. She didn't belong here any more than the magazine did.

An image of the plateau popped unbidden into her mind. She was sitting by the guelta with Max, drinking tea, listening to the bees, and wishing that she could stay there forever. Cairo stared unseeingly down at the magazine. The memory was so vivid that it hurt, and she had to wrench her mind away from it.

She was glad she had come with Max today, she told herself as she turned to the interview page. It had put paid once and for all to that bizarre idea that she might have been attracted to him, and reminded her just what her priorities were. She was going to pay off her father's debts and then settle down in the city, where she belonged, and she would never give Max or the desert so much as another thought.

Determined to believe it, Cairo adjusted her sunglasses and absorbed herself in the magazine, so successfully that she was not aware that Max had come round to stare at her until he spoke.

'Are you sure you're quite comfortable?' he asked with heavy irony, watching her incredulously over his door. There was a smudge of oil on his cheek and his eyes looked very light in his dark face.

'Yes, thank you,' said Cairo absently, her mind still on the winter collections. She had used to go to Paris and Milan to see the new designs; how long would it be before she could buy herself any new clothes? Recalling where she was, she laid the magazine down on her knees. 'Have you finished yet?'

For one terrifying moment, she thought Max was going to lean in and strangle her, but after a visible struggle he merely said through his teeth, 'No, I have *not* finished. It's a hundred and twenty degrees out here—hotter under the bonnet—and I've had to strip down the carburettor completely. If you think you can do it any faster with your renowned mechanical skills, you're very welcome to come and try, and *I'll* catch up on where the hemline is this year!'

'There's no need to jump down my throat!' With studied insolence, Cairo reopened her magazine. 'I'm sure you're going as fast as you can.'

The next instant, the magazine was torn from her hands as Max opened his door and lunged in. His face was suddenly very close to his own, and his grey-green eyes were ablaze with anger.

'I've had just about enough of you and your spoilt, selfish attitude! You don't appreciate how lucky you are to be seeing the desert like this. Oh, no! You're so narrow-minded that you'd really rather sit there and flick through a magazine that's so full of deceit and pretension that it probably means a lot to you. As long as you get your own way, nothing else matters, does it?' A muscle jumped furiously in his jaw. 'First of all you make me drag you with me up to the plateau, make it virtually impossible for me to do any work up there and now, when I'm sweating my guts out to get *you* to your precious locations, you have the nerve to sit there calmly reading that *tripe* and ask me if I've finished!'

Cairo's eyes narrowed to an intense, glittering green as she snatched back the magazine. '*You* were the one who wanted me to stay out of your way. I didn't realise that what you really wanted was for me to hover over you with a handkerchief to mop your brow and tell you how marvellous you are just because you're weird enough to like this place! Why should I appreciate the desert? It's hot and it's uncomfortable and it's boring, and I'm stuck in the middle of it with some latter-day Lawrence of Arabia who's so full of prejudices about London that it's almost funny and who dares to lecture *me* about being narrow-minded!'

'You'll be stuck for longer than you bargained for if you don't put that down right now and give me a hand,' Max threatened.

'Oh, for heaven's sake!' Cairo threw down the magazine and glared at him. 'What do you want me to do?'

'Just start her up—*if* it's not too much trouble for you.'

He went back to lean over the engine, and Cairo turned the ignition key when he gave her the order. The engine spluttered into miraculous life and there was a muffled shout from behind the bonnet.

'What?' she yelled over the racket.

'I said *turn her off*!' bellowed Max.

Cairo cut the engine and listened as the enveloping silence descended once more.

'All right,' he said. 'Come here.'

'Yes, *sir*,' she muttered, clambering down. 'What now?'

Max handed her some spanners. 'Hold these while I just tighten up the bolts.'

'Please?' she reminded him in a saccharine voice.

'How would you like me to drive off and leave you here?' Max directed his question pleasantly to the carburettor.

'You wouldn't dare!'

'I wouldn't push the point if I were you.' He thrust a spanner into her hand and helped himself to one of the others she was holding. 'The way I feel at the moment, it would be justifiable homicide and probably a great service to society in general!'

After a couple more adjustments, he slammed down the bonnet and told her curtly to get back in the jeep.

'I don't know why you're being so unpleasant,' said Cairo as they set off once more. 'I've told you, I haven't got anything to do with your wretched sister's problems.'

'It just seems very funny that Joanna's life is being turned upside-down again by a woman who is beautiful and heartless and in business with Piers... but not you, apparently. Tell me, how many beautiful, heartless women does Piers do business with?'

Cairo gritted her teeth. 'I am not having an affair with Piers. I never have and I never will. We're business partners and friends, that's all. Why won't you believe that?'

'You can't tell me a man like that could keep his hands off a girl like you!'

'You seem to be able to do it without any difficulty,' Cairo retorted before she could help herself.

'That's because I——' Max broke off as the jeep lunged to a halt, its wheels turning uselessly in the soft sand. Banging his fist against the steering-wheel, he swore fast and fluently.

'Now look what you've done!' Cairo accused him. 'We're bogged.'

Max slumped back in his seat. 'Marvellous! How did you work that one out?' he asked, rubbing his temples in frustration. 'This is all your fault.'

'*My* fault?' she squeaked indignantly. 'How does it get to be my fault? I wasn't driving.'

'If you hadn't been arguing, I might have been able to concentrate on what I was doing.'

'Who did you blame for all your problems until I came into your life?' Cairo asked acidly.

'I didn't have any problems until I met you!'

They jumped out of the jeep at the same time, both venting their feelings on the doors, and shouting across at each other childishly, 'Don't slam the door!'

The jeep was so deeply bogged that its chassis had buried into the sand. Max swore and kicked the wheel arch.

'That'll help,' said Cairo acidly.

He looked murder and threw a shovel towards her across the jeep. 'Get digging,' was all he said.

Cairo managed to sidestep the shovel and it landed with a muffled thud in the sand. Picking it up reluctantly, she began scraping the sand away from the front wheel on her side, until Max gave an exclamation of disgust.

'I said dig, not flick grains of sand around!' he said. 'We'll be here all day at the rate you're going. Put a bit of elbow grease into it!'

'Oh, shut up!' Cairo snapped, but she redoubled her efforts.

It was back-breaking work. For every shovel she scooped out, half of the fine sand seemed to trickle back into the hole from the sides, and they had to dig out the back wheels and under the chassis as well as the front. The back of Cairo's dress was drenched in sweat and the long skirts kept getting in the way as she bent with the shovel.

'Why didn't you stop as soon as you felt yourself driving into all this sand?' she demanded, wiping her scarlet face with the back of her arm.

'I would have done if you hadn't been yakking at me,' Max snarled. 'Keep digging!'

The sun beat down mercilessly, and the heat was making it hard to breathe. Cairo got herself into a rhythm—bend, scoop, bend, scoop—by chanting, 'I hate him, I hate him, I hate him,' under her breath, and it was the only thing that kept her going.

Max worked with characteristic efficiency, and finished digging out his side long before her. He could easily have come round to help dig on her side, but instead he stood, leaning on his shovel and watching her sweat with a sardonic expression on his face. Cairo would have died rather than ask him to help. She pressed her lips together firmly and bent over her shovel once more.

'I hate him, I hate him,' she muttered to herself.

By the time she was finished, she was utterly exhausted and could only collapse over her shovel, wondering if she would ever feel cool again. Max laid sand mats in front of the front wheels and went round the jeep lowering the tyre pressure.

'I should be able to drive her out now,' he said to Cairo, ignoring the fact that she was lying in an untidy heap on the sand, still gasping for breath. 'But I won't be able to stop until the ground feels firmer. If I lose momentum, she'll just dig in again.'

Cairo struggled into a sitting position. She couldn't go through that again! 'OK.'

'So you'll have to follow on foot with the sand mats,' he went on. 'I can't stop and pick you and them up, and I'm certainly not leaving them behind.'

'Why can't you stay behind?' Cairo demanded, using the shovel to haul herself to her feet.

'Because you're not experienced in desert driving,' Max explained with exaggerated patience. 'You'd probably bog us again.'

'I could hardly do worse than you so far,' she said waspishly.

'If you don't stop whingeing, I won't wait for you at all,' said Max, starting the engine to drown out any further protests.

Cairo blew the hair wearily off her forehead and watched the jeep drive up the sand mats and bowl off into the distance. Jamming her hat back on to her head, she hoisted a sand mat under each arm and began trudging after Max. The jeep shimmered through the heat haze like a mirage, never seeming to get any closer. Cairo was convinced that Max had driven further than he needed to just so that she would have a longer walk, and she was livid by the time she finally threw the sand mats into the back of the jeep.

'You did that deliberately!'

Max was leaning against her door, looking cool and relaxed. He raised an eyebrow at her. 'What?'

'You could have stopped at least half a mile back!' Cairo waved an arm behind her.

'I couldn't be sure of the sand,' Max said blandly. 'You might feel like digging out the jeep again, but I certainly don't.' He looked her up and down, from her battered hat and red face, to the limp dress caked with sand, and, to Cairo's fury, his light eyes creased with malicious amusement. 'You look rather hot, Cairo. Would you like a drink?'

He held the water bottle out, and she snatched it from his hand with a black look, but as their fingers touched, she felt such a shock of electric awareness that she nearly dropped it. Max had felt it too. She could see it in his eyes before he turned away, and her hand shook as she tipped back the water bottle. How could someone treat you as ruthlessly as Max had done all morning, and still be able to make you thrill at the merest brush of his fingers? It wasn't fair.

She could feel the awareness of that one brief touch simmering between them as they drove on over the sand. Just one touch, but it was enough to relight those other memories she had tried so hard to forget today: his hands against her skin, the taste of his mouth, the warm, smooth strength of his shoulders beneath her fingers.

Cairo slid a glance at Max under her lashes. He was scowling at the sand ahead, dark brows drawn together and jaw thrust forward. His mouth was set in a tight, angry line, and his hands gripped the steering-wheel so tightly that his knuckles stood out. What did he have to be so cross about? she wondered resentfully. She was the one who had had to trudge for miles in the burning heat with the sand mats.

Then she wondered what he would do if she leant across and kissed the corner of his mouth.

Cairo's lips tingled at the thought. Stop it, she told herself and wrenched her eyes away. You hate him. Don't even let yourself think about how it would feel.

The roar of the engine seemed to come from miles away. Cairo felt as if there was a pocket of silence enveloping her and Max. It was alive with hostility and a relentless tension that clawed at her nerves. She found that she was breathing very carefully, and although she kept her eyes rigidly ahead she was horribly aware of Max driving taut and controlled beside her. If she closed her eyes, the image of his mouth danced tauntingly behind her eyelids, and when she opened them again to stare at the empty horizon, the memory of his touch burned in her mind.

It was a relief when Max turned off the piste again and headed towards what appeared to be a solid wall of rock rising out of the desert. It gave Cairo something else to look at and something else to think about.

'Where are we going?'

'There's a guelta in here,' he said briefly, negotiating a path through an opening in the rocks. 'We'll spend the night by the water.' They emerged into an expanse of small boulders, bleached white by the sun, like a vast pebble beach adrift in the desert. The jeep bumped its way very slowly over the smooth stones until it dropped gratefully back on to smoother terrain and there, in front of her, was the pool, so deep and clear and green among the rocks that it looked almost unreal.

There were a couple of acacia trees near by, and an oleander bloomed at the edge, its pale pink flowers looking almost surreal against the bare backdrop of stone, but nothing else appeared to take advantage of the water. It just gleamed there mysteriously, with nothing to clutter its limpid depths. When Cairo peered in, she could see every pebble on the bottom.

Max was unloading the jeep and ignoring her. It was just as well she had brought that magazine, Cairo thought resentfully. After the way he had treated her all day, she wasn't going to sit around all evening and wait for him to notice her!

Hoisting out her own rucksack, she ostentatiously laid her sleeping mat as far away from Max's as she could. 'You'll be glad to know that I've got my own sleeping bag this time,' she couldn't resist saying to Max.

'I thought you didn't have one,' he said with a hard stare.

'I asked Bruce to lend me his,' she said, shaking the bag out and spreading it over the mat.

'I'm surprised you didn't ask him to come along and share it with you,' sneered Max.

Cairo's eyes narrowed dangerously. 'What do you mean by that?'

'Judging by the way you were fondling each other last night, I thought you might have tried it out with him already.'

'I suppose I should be grateful that you deigned to notice that I was there at all,' said Cairo in a voice that dripped ice. 'But I was certainly not *fondling*, and nor was Bruce.'

'It looked like fondling to me. I've never seen such a revolting display!' Max yanked savagely at the cord of his rucksack and pulled out his own sleeping bag, which he threw on to the mat.

'You'd think anyone behaving in a vaguely civilised manner was revolting,' said Cairo, too angry to notice that she was emptying her pack quite unnecessarily.

'You call that *civilised*? I can think of plenty of terms for the way you were batting your eyelashes and fawning all over Bruce, but civilised isn't one of them! The poor man didn't know what had hit him,' Max jeered. 'Of course, I might have known you wanted something. All that effort just to get a sleeping bag off him ... or was it something else?' he added nastily.

Cairo had kept her back pointedly turned, but now she swung round. 'It wasn't anything! I happened to be enjoying Bruce's company, which is more than I can say about *yours*.'

'I didn't get that impression when you were snuggling up under my sleeping bag,' Max taunted her. 'Or was that just you behaving in a civilised way?'

Provoked beyond endurance, Cairo advanced on him, green eyes blazing. 'I wouldn't waste my time being civilised to you! I've never met anyone so arrogant and inconsiderate and *insufferable*, and if you think I'd ever go *near* you unless I was absolutely desperate, you must need your head examined! I can hardly bear to touch you!'

'Oh, yes?' snarled Max, grabbing her roughly and swinging her up into his arms before she realised what was happening. 'The only thing I need my head examining for is ever agreeing to have anything to do with you!'

'Put me down,' ordered Cairo as he strode over towards the pool.

Max stood at the very edge of a boulder and gave her a ferocious smile. 'Of course. You can't bear me touching you, can you? Well, we can soon do something about that,' he said, and threw her out into the deepest part of the pool.

Her mouth still open in outrage, Cairo plunged into the water with a tremendous splash that shattered the desert calm. It couldn't have been all that cold, but the contrast between the water and the hot air gave it the impact of diving into a pool of ice, and she was beside herself with shock and fury as she surfaced.

'You . . . you . . . !' She spluttered and coughed in frustration, unable to think of a word bad enough. 'I hate you!' she managed to shout childishly in the end.

'Good,' said Max with a nasty grin from the boulder. 'That makes it mutual.'

Cairo's flailing feet found the pebble bottom as she struggled towards the edge, hampered by her sodden dress. When she got to the boulder she was standing up to her chest, and she reached up a hand to let Max pull her out.

He took it instinctively, leaning forward. Cairo's eyes gleamed a sudden vivid green, and with one sharp, vicious tug she pulled him off balance and brought him crashing into the water beside her.

CHAPTER EIGHT

STAGGERING in the backsplash, Cairo backed away as Max surfaced, his hair sleek and wet.

'Why, you little——!' he grated, and reached for her, but she fell back out of his reach.

'You started it,' she pointed out. The bodice of her dress clung to the curve of her breast, and she tugged at it in a vain effort to make it less revealing. Her hair hung in dripping rat's tails of dark gold, and drops of water clung to her eyelashes.

Max flicked his head to get the water out of his eyes. They caught the sunlight reflecting off the water, and looked even more startlingly light than usual in his dark face. His khaki shirt was damp and dark, stuck to his broad chest like a second skin.

Standing chest-deep in the desert pool, they glared at each other and then, quite suddenly, the accumulated tension of the day snapped at the absurdity of it all, and they both began to laugh.

Their laughter rang across the water and echoed out over the bleached rocks. One by one, the tight ropes of strain that had bound them all day loosened their grip and fell away altogether as they threw their heads back and laughed and laughed.

'You are without doubt the most infuriating woman I have ever met,' said Max, gasping for breath, still laughing, and he lunged towards her, dragging her back down beneath the water.

Cairo was ready this time. The first chill of the water had passed, leaving her cool and exhilarated, and she closed her mouth and eyes as she sank so that when they surfaced, shaking their hair out of their eyes, they were both still grinning like lunatics.

141

They were standing quite close together, smiling into each other's eyes, when for some indefinable reason the atmosphere changed abruptly again. Their smiles faded slowly as their eyes held and there was a long moment of silence.

Cairo could feel the drips running down between her breasts. The late afternoon sun was warm on her back and the water cool and silky against her skin. It rocked around them and then steadied slowly as the last ripples shimmered across the surface towards the edge of the pool.

She looked into Max's eyes, and the expression she read there set her heart thudding with a slow, reverberating, almost painful beat. The vast landscape shrank until there was nothing but the two of them, staring at each other in the cool desert pool, the air tightening between them, shortening their breath and making it difficult to breathe. For Cairo, time itself seemed to unwind with each long, slow beat of her pulse until Max reached out for her and it stopped altogether.

He held her face between his hands, his palms hard against her soft cheeks. Cairo could feel their cool strength flowing through her, and she began to tremble, but she made no move to step away. All she could do was look into his eyes, her own a deep, intense green, the pupils dark and dilated with a desire that could be denied no longer.

She never knew how long they stood there, or which of them it was that made the first move. Did she step towards him, or did he pull her roughly into his arms? All she knew was that the stillness and the silence and the deep, painful tremble of desire were suddenly unbearable and as the spell that had held them immobile snapped, she found herself in Max's arms, returning his hungry kisses with a sort of desperation.

Her hands spread across his chest and then slid round him as she strained closer, melted against the hard, exciting body. Max still cupped her face greedily between long fingers, holding her as if he feared that she might pull away, but her lips were warm and eager beneath his, and he let his hands slide round to the nape of her neck and then down her spine to hold her closer still.

Their clothes were so wet that they might as well have been naked. Cairo could feel the heat and demand of his body, and she pulled his shirt out of his trousers so that she could slip her hands beneath and glory in the feel of his wet, sleek, smooth, firm back, in the way his muscles flexed at the touch of her hungry fingers.

'Cairo,' said Max, with a rather shaky laugh as they broke apart for breath. His arms held her tightly, and he bent his head again almost immediately to burn kisses along her jaw. 'How can you do this to me?' he murmured against her ear, kissing the soft skin just beneath the lobe, and Cairo shivered in response.

'Do what?' she asked with difficulty, and tipped her head with a gasp of inarticulate pleasure as his lips drifted down her throat, setting her skin afire with exquisite sensations.

'One moment I want to murder you, and the next...'

'Yes?' she whispered huskily. Her arms slid out from beneath his shirt and wound around his neck. 'Yes?' she asked again, teasing kisses at the corner of his mouth, smiling against his rough male jaw because she knew the answer. 'What do you want to do next?'

Max began to pull her over towards the shallow edge of the pool, where the pebbles shelved up a narrow beach. 'I'll show you,' he said, and his voice was very deep and warm with promise.

The water rocked as they waded through the shallows, throwing shifting reflections of light over their faces, and streamed from their clothes as they clambered out on to the beach. Neither of them even noticed. As soon as they reached dry ground, Max pulled Cairo hard against him once more, and she lifted her face to meet his kiss.

'Show me now,' she murmured against his lips.

Max's mouth was hot and demanding on hers, and as the desire grew between them, threatening to spin out of control, so did their kisses become more frantic, the need more intense.

Fumbling with the buttons at the front of her dress, Max kissed her face, her throat, the curve of her breast as he managed to undo the top one, cursing under his breath as the second one proved more intractable. In the end Cairo helped him, although her fingers were hardly more steady than his own, and when they were all undone she stood still and quivering with anticipation.

Max took a sharp breath as he looked down into her face, then, taking the sodden material of the dress between his fingers, he peeled it slowly off her shoulders, past her waist, over the slim hips, following its path with hot, lingering kisses against her wet skin, until it lay in a puddle of water around her feet.

Cairo's fingers tangled and clung in his hair, as if to anchor herself. She was almost frightened by the gusts of sensation that shook her with every touch of Max's mouth, by the aching fire of need that twisted tighter and tighter within her until it was so acute that it veered on the edge of pain.

Max began to straighten, and Cairo shuddered as his mouth teased a trail of fire up her flat stomach. She was completely naked now, and his hands slid insistently over her curves, making her gasp with excitement.

'Shall I show you more?' he murmured hoarsely as he reached the pulse beating wildly at the base of her throat. His breathing was ragged, and Cairo arched her body, scarcely conscious of anything but his brown fingers at her breast, his lips drifting tantalisingly below her ear.

'Yes,' she gasped. Her mouth was so dry with excitement that she could hardly speak. Disentangling her fingers from his hair, she began to unbutton his shirt with fierce concentration. Max stood quite still until all the buttons were undone, looking down into her face with an intent smile in his eyes. She let him drag the wet shirt off himself when she had finished and their eyes met in acknowledgement of shared need as it dropped to the ground.

Cairo's eyes were very green. She spread her hands wide against his bare chest, and let them slide slowly down to the buckle of his belt. Leaning forward, she touched her lips to his throat, and then to each of his nipples.

'Yes,' she whispered against his skin, and this time it sounded more like a plea. 'Show me more.'

When he was as naked as she, Max lifted Cairo in his arms and carried her across to his sleeping mat. They sank down on it together, their hands moving hungrily over each other, their kisses newly urgent, their bodies glorying at the new awareness of skin on skin.

'Cairo.' Max murmured her name against her breast and she thrilled at the note in his voice. His body was hard and insistent on hers, and she arched her head back.

'Yes . . . yes,' she said, almost sobbing, not knowing what she meant, knowing only that the need was unendurable. She turned her head feverishly, digging her fingers into his shoulders until Max lifted his head at her unspoken plea.

He braced himself on his elbows, he held her face in his hands to look down into her eyes. 'Cairo,' he said again, and his voice was a caress. The sun was sinking rapidly, the late, slanting rays burnishing her skin with an unearthly red-gold light.

Lowering his head at last, Max kissed her mouth once more, then again and again. Cairo wrapped herself around him with a cry of release as at last he sheathed his hardness in the softness of her body, and they began to move together in a timeless, instinctive rhythm. As one, they gave themselves up to the whirl of sensation, to the soaring, gasping excitement of touch and taste and feel.

Max buried his face against Cairo's neck, and she clung to him as the passion that burnt between them scorched her senses and pushed them remorselessly higher, and higher, and higher still, until there was no further to go. For one heart-stopping moment, Cairo hesitated at the very brink of sensation, but Max was with her, and together they took the final step, letting their senses dissolve in an explosion of ecstasy, and calling each other's name as they spiralled down at last into the warm afterglow of fulfilment.

Later, much later, Cairo opened her eyes. Somehow she expected everything to be changed, but the desert was still there, the pool still gleamed quiet and mysterious in the fading light. Over the horizon, the sky was streaked with fiery red, and the stones which had seemed so white and bleached before now glowed in sunset.

Max still lay heavily on top of her, but Cairo didn't mind. She wanted to stay there forever, with her senses singing and her body entangled with his.

Her fingers slid luxuriously down his arm, loving the feel of him, and he turned his head and kissed her neck before raising himself on one elbow.

'All right?' he asked quietly. He tucked a stray hair away from her forehead, and stroked his thumb along her cheekbone, letting his hand linger against her glowing face.

Cairo nodded. 'Much better,' she smiled up at him, and he smiled back as the memory of what they had shared shimmered between them.

She had never seen him smile like that before, not with that warmth in his eyes and that light in his face, and her heart clenched at the realisation of quite what he meant to her.

I love you. She wanted to say it, but for some reason she hesitated, unwilling to spoil the moment with doubts or expectations. For now, it was enough that he was there, smiling at her like that.

'I'm sorry I was such a brute to you today,' Max said, suddenly serious, his hand tightening against her cheek.

'You were a pig,' said Cairo, but she was smiling as she linked her arms around his neck. 'I'm sure I deserved it, though!'

Max laughed and kissed her. 'You did!' He got to his feet and reached down a hand to pull her up. 'Come on, time for another swim.'

'I'd like to go in the shallow end this time,' Cairo said as they made their way back down to the pool, and then shrieked as Max swept her up into his arms and made as if to throw her into the depths after all. 'Don't!' she said, clutching at him and trying to look threatening at the same time.

Max was grinning. 'Ask me nicely!'

'Please don't,' she coaxed, tightening her arms around his neck and kissing his ear, then his cheek, then the corner of his mouth.

Turning his head, he met her lips, and they kissed as he let her go, letting her slide slowly down his body before setting her feet on the pebble beach. 'You should have asked me like that before!'

'I don't think it would have had the slightest effect,' said Cairo frankly. 'You were in such a filthy mood that nothing less than dumping me into freezing water would have satisfied you.'

'Whereas you were so sweet-tempered that you would have done anything I asked, I suppose?'

Cairo laughed and took his hand as they waded into the pool. 'I was only cross because you were cross,' she explained.

'And I was only cross because you were so infuriating,' Max retorted virtuously.

The water was cool and refreshing against their flushed skin. Cairo grimaced at the temperature and she sank up to her neck, but when the first shock was past she could feel sheer exhilaration flooding through her. She swam exuberantly across to the other side of the pool to warm herself up and then back to Max, shaking the hair out of her eyes, her smile gleaming in the last of the light.

'Was I really so infuriating?' she asked, treading water. Surely she hadn't been *that* bad?

Max drew her towards him and let his hands slide possessively over her sleek body. 'Yes,' he said, and laughed at her outraged expression. His grip tightened as she made as if to pull away and she soon gave up the attempt as he held her close. Their legs entangled, and Cairo put her arms around his neck and kissed him. The kiss went on and on, until they submerged, still kissing, and surfaced, breathless and laughing, to kiss again.

Afterwards, they made a fire with some dead acacia branches, and heated up a spicy lamb stew that Max had brought. Cairo stirred the stew and was filled with a deep, wordless happiness whenever Max touched her casually, resting his hand at the nape of her neck or letting it linger down her spine.

I love you. Why hadn't she said it? Because whenever she wondered whether Max might love her too, doubt clawed at her mind. He had had plenty of opportunity to say so, but he hadn't. He desired her, she knew that, but it wasn't quite the same as love. Max was a loner, and he was unlikely to change his life for a woman, no matter how much he wanted her. And if he wouldn't change, he wouldn't make false promises either. Cairo didn't want to see the apprehension in his eyes when he realised that for her it was more than just physical desire. She wanted him, yes, more than she had thought possible, but she loved him and needed him too.

How had she fallen so hopelessly in love with Max? He was all wrong for her, she thought desperately, but it didn't change the fact. He was the only man she would ever love like this, she knew it in her bones. Cairo remembered wryly how she had read that magazine while Max had been fixing the jeep, how she had convinced herself that she was longing to go home. What would home be without Max?

They ate the stew as the stars appeared in their millions, massing together in the deep blue velvet of the sky until Cairo grew dizzy watching them. It was absolutely quiet. No distant sound of cars or people, not even the surreptitious night sounds she remembered from the plateau. There was only Max breathing quietly beside her as she leant against him, and the occasional crack as a rock shattered in the falling temperature.

She wouldn't be able to bear the city after this, Cairo thought with an edge of panic, and then following swiftly on the thought was the cold realisation that she would have to bear it. She couldn't just give it all up and stay here with Max, even if she had thought he wanted her to. There was still her father to consider.

Cairo didn't want to imagine what Max would think if he knew the truth about her father. She knew how he felt about corruption, knew that he would be disgusted if he ever found out the real reason she was so desperate to complete this job. She never wanted to see the contempt in his eyes for her father, a man he would consider guilty and corrupt, a man who was for her only the other man who had ever been the centre of her world. Her father had done everything for her, and she couldn't abandon him now, not even for Max.

She turned her head slightly to look up at him. His face was etched in moonlight as he stared into the distance absorbed in his own thoughts. Every line of his face was achingly familiar, and her heart clenched as her eyes rested on his mouth and remembered how it had felt against her skin.

As if he was aware of the renewed desire that shuddered down her spine, Max's arm tightened around her and he looked down into her eyes. 'You're very quiet,' he said. 'What are you thinking about?'

For a brief moment, Cairo hesitated, wondering if she should tell him after all, but the night was too perfect.

She would think about the future tomorrow; for tonight, the present was enough.

So instead of opening her heart to him, she turned within the circle of his arm and knelt so that their faces were on a level. 'I was just thinking,' she murmured, pressing tantalising butterfly kisses along his jaw towards his mouth, 'that I won't need Bruce's sleeping bag after all.'

'So you won't,' said Max with a smile, and pulled her down with him on to the mat.

This time their lovemaking was exquisitely slow, a languorous rediscovery of joy without the wild urgency that had driven them before. Afterwards, Cairo lay curled against him, content to listen to his steady breathing, and when she was sure he was asleep, she pressed her lips to his shoulder, and whispered, 'I love you,' against his skin.

She woke to the feel of hard hands drifting over her slender curves, lighting a slow-burning fuse of desire, and she stretched luxuriously beneath them. The sun was still hidden behind the rocky crags to the east, but the air was suffused with the pearly dawn light.

'I thought you were never going to wake up,' he pretended to complain, dropping slow kisses along the breathtaking line of her clavicle.

Cairo stretched again and smiled sleepily up at him, surprising a blaze of expression in his eyes. She slipped her hands around his neck. 'I'm awake now,' she said.

'It's late,' said Max, trying to sound stern, but his touch was anything but stern as his hand slid lovingly along her thigh, curving over her hip and caressing her breast. 'We ought to get up.'

'Ought we?' Cairo let her fingers drift enticingly down his body.

'Yes,' he said unconvincingly.

'Right now?' she murmured, letting her hands work their own magic on him, and shifting her body beneath his in wanton invitation.

'Yes,' said Max again, and then spoiled the effect by pressing her back down on to the sleeping mat. 'Well, perhaps not quite yet,' he amended as he found her mouth with his own.

'Let's stay another day,' he suggested as they lay entwined in the shallows after another swim. Cairo was tingling all over from the invigorating water and the aftermath of their lovemaking, and she was unprepared for his suggestion.

Stay another day. It wasn't the same as *don't go*, but it was heaven all the same. Another day alone with Max. It wasn't much to ask.

But she was so far behind schedule. Piers and Haydn Deane would be expecting her back tomorrow, and it would still take her several days to clear the permits with officials in Menesset and make all the other arrangements about accommodation and transport.

'I can't,' she said drearily as the dream vanished. 'I've got to get back.'

Max released her abruptly. 'Why? Bored already?'

'No!' Cairo sat up, chilled at the expression on his face. 'No, Max, it's not that. You know it isn't. I've just got to get this job finished.'

'Forget about the job,' he said, getting to his feet and stepping into his trousers which had been drying on a rock next to Cairo's dress. 'Surely you've seen enough of the desert to know that this isn't just a backdrop for some stupid advertisement in a magazine that's going to be flicked through and immediately forgotten?' He pulled Cairo up and ran his hands tantalisingly over her shoulders. 'We'll stay here today and you can send them a telex from the camp tomorrow telling them you can't find anywhere suitable.'

'Max, I can't,' said Cairo in despair, torn by her loyalty and the longing that his touch always roused in her. 'There are people relying on me.'

His hands dropped from her shoulders. 'Like Piers, for instance?'

'Yes, Piers, among others,' she said, trying to stay calm and reasonable.

Max wasn't even making the effort. 'What is it about that man that makes women make fools of themselves for him?' he demanded bitterly, shrugging on his shirt and beginning to roll up his sleeves.

'I haven't made a fool of myself,' said Cairo grittily. 'Stop blaming Piers or me for your sister's problems. I don't know what the situation is between them, but Piers has always been a friend to me. A *friend*,' she stressed, 'not a lover. It was Piers who gave me a chance to set up in business when no one else would.'

'It was also Piers who sent you off completely unprepared into the desert when if he'd had any sense of decency he'd have come himself. He's using you, Cairo, just as he seems to use every other woman he comes across.'

Cairo snatched up her dress and pulled it over her head. She had lost the battle to hold her temper. 'What would you know about it?' she demanded, buttoning it up all wrong. 'You don't even know Piers. I do, and even if he *was* using me, which he isn't, I said I would do this job and I'm not going back on my word!'

'I can't believe that this famous job of yours really means more to you than all that we have here,' said Max, baffled and angry.

'It doesn't.'

'Then prove it by staying another day. Prove it by not bringing the shoot here.'

Cairo pressed the heels of her hands against her eyes. 'Max, I can't.'

'Why not?'

He wouldn't understand about the chains of guilt and loyalty and love that bound her to her father. He wouldn't understand how much it had meant when Piers had offered her a way to make some money at last after the bleak months of rejection.

'I . . . can't explain,' she said dully.

Max's face closed. 'You don't need to explain. I can work it out for myself. You can't wait to get back to so-called civilisation, can you? You can wear your make-up every day, and spend your day going through your Filofax and your nights at parties having meaningless conversations with meaningless people. You can tell them all about the little fling you had in the desert. That should give them all a good laugh!'

'Oh, what's the point in arguing?' Cairo cried bitterly. 'You won't listen anyway. You're too pigheaded and prejudiced to see anything but your own point of view!' She marched over to her pack and began stuffing her things back in it. 'If you ask me, you've just got a chip on your shoulder because of your mother. It's not my fault she left you! You think that everyone's like her, but they're not, and I'm not either! *You're* the one with the problem. It might surprise you to know that cities are full of kind, decent people who manage to cope with life without cutting themselves off in the desert.'

Max was looking white about the mouth. 'Well, you'd better go back there if it's all so wonderful,' he said harshly, and threw his pack into the back of the jeep.

They drove straight back to the camp in bitter silence. Max sat grim-faced beside her, and Cairo was too hurt and angry to relent. He was so unreasonable! Did he really expect her to drop everything just to spend an extra day with him? He hadn't mentioned staying any longer, she remembered bleakly. She didn't mean that much to him.

Everything had been so perfect last night. How had it all gone so wrong, so quickly? Cairo's heart felt as if it were cracking, splintering into a thousand pieces of ice, but she wouldn't let herself cry. Her jaw ached with the effort and a dull pain thudded behind her eyes.

She loved him so much. Her body burned with the need to reach across and touch him, and she had to sit with her hands gripped so tightly together that the knuckles showed white. It would never have worked, she tried to tell herself. Max's reaction this morning had proved that. He would always associate her with the kind of life his mother led. Staying another day wouldn't have made any difference.

If she had agreed to stay, they wouldn't have been driving back in this cold silence. Cairo couldn't stop imagining what they might have been doing, if only she had said yes. They would have found some shade among the rocks, and thrown down the mats. They would have talked and touched, and when the heat of the day was passed they would have made their way back to the pool to swim in its cool waters and make love once more as the sun went down. Cairo's body throbbed, so vividly she could imagine it. She knew exactly how Max's hard body would have felt beneath her fingers, how his lips would have felt against her skin.

All she had had to do was say that she would stay another day.

Cairo stared unseeingly through the cracked windscreen, her green eyes dark with regret. Another day, her heart whispered. What difference would it have made?

It would have made it even harder to say goodbye.

As they drove into the camp, Max spoke for the first time. He stopped the jeep outside the guest quarters, but didn't turn off the engine. 'You'd better get your stuff out of the back,' he said tonelessly. 'I'm going on.'

'Where are you going?'

'Nowhere that has any interest to you,' he said in the same expressionless voice.

Cairo hauled her pack out of the jeep and dropped it on the ground. 'I suppose you're going to commune with some of your precious rocks?' she said, unable to help herself, and Max was provoked out of his careful control.

'They'll be better company than you,' he snapped.

'They're welcome to you!' Cairo made a point of slamming her door shut. 'I'm going back to the real world!'

'You're welcome to each other,' snarled Max, shoving the jeep into gear, and he drove off with a screech of tyres, leaving Cairo coughing in the dust cloud he left behind him, and blaming the drifting sand for the tears in her eyes.

CHAPTER NINE

PIERS was elated when Cairo showed him the photographs. 'This is exactly what they wanted,' he enthused as he spread them out over the desk. 'Those rocks against the sand will make a spectacular backdrop for the shoot.'

Cairo thought of Max and her heart contracted. The desert isn't just a backdrop, he had said. Piers would never understand that.

She stared down at the photographs. They looked so unreal against the clutter of the desk. There was the rock she had sat on while she waited for Max to reappear. She could visualise him so clearly that she half expected him to step out of the picture, and she closed her eyes in sudden anguish. If only she could forget! Every detail of the day she had taken the pictures was etched on her memory: the arguments with Max, digging out the jeep, the icy water closing over her head as he threw her in the pool, Max throwing back his head and laughing, his eyes reflecting the light from the water, his hands as they peeled the sodden dress from her shoulders . . .

Cairo moved abruptly away from the desk. 'Do you think Haydn Deane will mind that it's not actually the plateau?'

'Not if we present it to them properly. This looks like a great location you've found, and they're bound to be impressed by your efficiency in making all the arrangements beforehand.' Piers gathered up the photographs and banged them between his hands on the desk to make a neat pile. 'You've done a great job, Cairo. I told you it would be easy!'

Cairo thought of the long climb up the plateau, of Max's grey face as he clutched the hand the snake had bitten, of the dull ache in her heart, but she said nothing. There was nothing to say.

'You don't seem your usual sparky self,' Piers commented in concern. 'Are you all right?'

'I'm fine,' said Cairo with an over-bright smile. 'Just a bit tired, that's all.'

She couldn't remember much of the last few days in Menesset. Moving jerkily like a robot, she had visited officials, dealt with interminable red tape, booked hotel rooms and arranged for three vehicles with drivers to take the whole party out to the location. Once or twice she had caught sight of her reflection as she nodded and smiled and charmed her way past officials, and she marvelled that she could look so normal when her heart was breaking.

'So you'll be OK to see Haydn Deane this afternoon?' said Piers with undisguised relief. 'They've been champing at the bit waiting for you to get back. They want to get everything moving as quickly as possible. It's just as well you didn't stay any longer.'

'Just as well,' Cairo echoed desolately, pushing aside the memory of that morning at the pool when Max had asked her to stay another day. She walked over to the window and stood looking down at the street. The pavements were thronged with people, their umbrellas up against the spring rain, and the traffic was banked up impatiently behind the lights. This had been home before she went to Shofrar, but now she longed for the vast skies and empty horizons of the desert with an almost physical ache.

Cairo turned to face Piers once more. 'Piers, do you know a girl called Joanna?' she asked on the spur of the moment.

His face lit up. 'Joanna Haddington? Do you know her?'

'Not exactly. I met her brother in Shofrar.'

'That'll be the famous Max, I suppose,' said Piers a little glumly. 'Joanna adores him, but it doesn't sound as if he approves much of me. I gather he practically brought her up after their parents split, and he's the one she turns to for advice. I'm not quite sure why; apparently he's filthy rich but opted out of things here to go and work in the desert. He only comes home to see Joanna occasionally. He's obviously a bit of an eccentric.'

'He's not an eccentric!' said Cairo, nettled. A vision of Max rose before her, silhouetted against the glare with his old hat, eyes narrowed as he looked towards the horizon, and her heart cracked. 'He's the sanest man I know.'

Piers looked unconvinced. 'I just wish Joanna wasn't under his influence quite so much. He's not much use to her out in Shofrar, and besides, she's got me to look after her now.'

'That doesn't sound like you, Piers,' said Cairo. 'I've never even heard you mention Joanna before! I thought you were the love 'em and leave 'em type?'

'Not any more.' His handsome face lit up with boyish enthusiasm. 'We've been trying to keep it a secret, but I'd marry Joanna and settle down tomorrow if I could. I've never met anyone like her before. She's so sweet and gentle. She's so different from the other girls I used to go out with. They were like you, could look after themselves, but Joanna's not like that. She's the sort of girl you want to protect.'

Joanna was a lucky girl, Cairo couldn't help reflecting. She wished she brought out the protective instincts in men. She was tired of looking after herself.

'If you feel like that, why don't you get married?' she asked Piers.

'Joanna went through a pretty ghastly divorce last year, so she's still vulnerable. I don't want to rush her into anything. Everyone would assume I'd just married her for her money, like her last brute of a husband did.' Piers paced around the room. 'That's one of the reasons I was so anxious to make a success of this business. I want to show Joanna that she can trust me, that I'm not just a loser who'll never have any money of his own,' he said, smacking his fist into his hand. 'If Haydn Deane OK this new location of yours this afternoon, we'll be on our way. I haven't told Joanna much about our partnership yet,' he went on. 'I wanted to wait until I could be sure it was going to be a success.'

He would have told Joanna just enough to make her suspicious, Cairo thought wryly. She had probably followed Piers one day, had seen him meet her, perhaps disappear into the office with her, and had obviously drawn her own conclusions. Why hadn't Joanna just asked Piers instead of writing to Max about her suspicions? Cairo wondered exasperatedly. She would have saved a lot of trouble all round if she'd used her head for a change!

Cairo was nervous as they waited to see two of the associates at Haydn Deane that afternoon, but, as Piers had predicted, they were delighted with the photographs and were soon taking all the credit for deciding that the plateau wouldn't have been a suitable location after all. They were even more impressed by the detailed arrangements Cairo had made, and asked her to travel back with the group to make sure everything went as planned.

'We'd like to move as soon as possible on this one,' they said. 'The clients want to use Jasmin, but she's only available for a few days in two weeks' time. Can you firm up all the arrangements for then?'

Cairo nodded, but her heart sank at the news that she was going to have to deal with one of London's top models. Jasmin was so well known that she never used a surname, and she had a reputation for being difficult. Cairo dreaded to think how she was going to react to conditions in the desert.

Piers was beaming as they left, jubilant at the prospect of having their fee paid at last. The associates had also dropped some heavy hints about some other jobs in the pipeline, and he was bursting with enthusiasm.

'We're on our way!' he said to Cairo, sweeping her into a hug. 'I can't wait to tell Joanna! Thanks to you, we've got the first job in the bag. There'll be no stopping us now, Cairo, just you wait and see. Our troubles are over!'

His might be, Cairo thought bitterly, but hers were only just beginning. She had to learn to live without Max.

On the flight from Shofrar, she had told herself that once she was back in the routine at home it would be easy to put him behind her, but the differences only served to emphasise how much she missed him. She missed his loose easy stride and the way he wore his hat. She missed the acidity in his voice and the exasperation in his eyes when she made him cross. She missed the air of cool self-sufficiency that made her feel so safe. Most of all, she missed the touch of his lean, hard body and the way he had smiled before he kissed her.

Cairo tried to sound enthusiastic about the prospects of the business when she went to visit her father. The fee for their first job would enable her to pay back the loan her godmother had made, and after that any money she earned could go towards paying off what remained of his debts. 'It'll take some time, though,' she warned, unwilling to get his hopes up too high. 'But if things go as well as Piers seems to think they will, we could pay off quite a few this year.'

Jeremy Kingswood looked at his daughter. There was a fine-drawn look of exhaustion about her and her bare face was burnt brown by the desert sun but she was somehow more beautiful than before. He frowned as he saw the unhappiness shadowing the huge green eyes.

'You look tired,' he said quietly. 'This past year hasn't been easy for you, has it?' Leaning forward, he took her hand and squeezed it. 'I'm sorry, darling, I never wanted you to have to worry like this. I wish you'd give up this idea of paying off the debts. Now that we've sold everything, there aren't that many left. I'll manage somehow.'

Cairo put her free hand over his. 'You looked after me for all those years, Daddy. Now it's my turn.' She saw the emotion quiver on his face, and smiled at him, trying to turn the conversation to more cheerful channels. 'I'm lucky to have such an interesting job. Not everyone gets to jaunt off to the desert as part of their work!'

Jeremy Kingswood contented himself with squeezing her hand, and followed her lead. 'What was it like?'

Cairo thought of the stark grandeur of the plateau and the fierce light, the perfect curve of the dunes and the shadows at sunset. She thought of the guelta where the bees had hummed in the cedar trees, and the clear green waters among the bleached stones. She didn't think she would ever be able to explain what the desert had been like.

'It was very hot,' she said. 'Hot and empty. Lots of rocks and lots of sand.'

Her father was looking horrified. 'Poor Cairo! You're such a city girl, too! You must have hated it!'

The green eyes darkened with memory. 'I didn't hate it,' she said, and to her horror, her voice cracked. 'I loved it.'

Cairo couldn't believe how many people it appeared were essential to take a few simple photographs. They would need at least another car, she realised when Haydn Deane sent her the final list of personnel, and she would just have to hope that there were more hotel rooms available when they got there. At least this wasn't the tourist season.

She was longing to see the desert again, but dreading taking other people back to share her memories, and when she met the group at the airport before the flight her heart sank even further. They were exactly the kind of people Max would most despise, gushing and affected, littering their conversations with 'darling' and extravagant gestures.

The model, Jasmin, drew all eyes. She was tall and exotically dark, with a wide, dramatic red mouth and sultry brown eyes. There was a steamy, smouldering quality about her that made Cairo feel like a Brownie. She had recognised her at once, of course, had even seen her at a few parties, but she was unprepared for the dislike she felt when she finally met her.

Jasmin was a star, and made sure everyone knew it. Her trademark pout could sell anything, but her temperament was notorious, and Haydn Deane was well aware of what it would cost if she were to walk out on the shoot. Jasmin must be placated at all costs, they insisted, so, when Jasmin made no secret of the fact that she despised Cairo quite as much as Cairo loathed her, Cairo just had to hold her tongue, grit her teeth and remember her father's debts.

Her stomach churned as the plane touched down in Menesset. She was back in the same country as Max. She knew that the chance of seeing him was remote, but still her eyes searched the streets for the familiar jeep as a convoy of taxis took the group into the town. What would she do if she saw him? What could she say?

Ushering the group into the hotel, she tried to ignore their exclamations of horror at the shabby furnishings and lack of bar.

'I'm used to five-star hotels,' Jasmin stormed. 'My agent never told me I'd have to put up with cockroaches in the bedrooms! And there's no bathroom in my room!'

She had reacted in much the same way when she had first come to Menesset, Cairo remembered. That was before she'd met Max, before she'd learnt that there were more important things to care about. 'There are showers at the end of each corridor,' she said, trying to keep her voice even. 'I'm sorry if it's not what you're used to, but I'm afraid this is the best hotel in Menesset. It's only for two nights.'

When she had quietened them all down, she went into her own room and shut the door gratefully behind her.

Crossing over to the window, she opened the shutters and stood looking out over the geometric huddle of windowless, whitewashed houses with their flat roofs and tiny courtyards.

An unnatural hush seemed to settle over the town as the light faded rapidly from the sky. Cairo watched a blue-robed figure duck out of a doorway to avoid knocking the huge *shesh* he wore wrapped around his head, and stride off towards the marketplace. The easy walk reminded her of Max, and the jab of longing was so sharp that she winced and rubbed her hand over her heart as if to soothe it. How long was she going to have to live with this raw sense of need?

Outside, the stillness seemed to intensify for the instant before a loudspeaker crackled into life near by and the mournful wail of the muezzin began, calling the faithful to prayer. As if at a signal, the silence lifted. Pans clattered, somewhere a dog barked, voices were raised in machine-gun chatter and normal life was resumed.

Cairo's eyes blurred with tears. How could normal life resume for her when all she wanted was a man who lived alone in the desert, a man with cool eyes and a touch that set her heart racing?

There was chaos the next morning when the vehicles arrived. It was immediately obvious that they could not all squeeze into the two cars that she had ordered, and the group stood around complaining about their rooms while Cairo embarked on a tortured conversation with the drivers to find out whether they could get hold of a third car. She had to struggle to make sense of their fractured French, and after a while Jasmin heaved an ostentatious sigh.

'This is obviously going to take all morning,' she said scathingly. 'I thought all this had been arranged in advance?'

'I made the arrangements before another four people were added to the original list,' Cairo pointed out through clenched teeth.

'If you'd known anything about the business, you'd have guessed that the numbers would change,' Jasmin said with a shrug. 'I've no intention of hanging around while you sort this out. I'm going for a walk.' She strolled off, patently enjoying all the attention her dramatic looks always created.

Cairo pressed her lips together, counted to ten and turned back to the drivers. She had just managed to establish that there was indeed a third car available, when Jasmin reappeared. Cairo had her back to her, and didn't see her at first until the drivers' look of blatant admiration made her turn round.

Max was standing there, with Jasmin hanging on his arm.

Cairo felt as if she'd been hit by a sledgehammer. Her heart seemed to stop, and then jolt into frantic life while she struggled for breath, and she clutched the clipboard to her chest like a lifeline.

He looked exactly the same. The same cool, guarded expression, the same air of coiled strength. Cairo couldn't take her eyes off him. She seethed with conflicting emotions: shock, incredulous joy, and a burning resentment that he could stand there and look as if he hardly recognised her.

Jasmin seemed to be talking from a great distance, but there was no mistaking the smug look on her face. 'It's all right, darling,' she said patronisingly to Cairo. 'You can stop panicking about another car. I've found a gallant knight to rescue us from our dilemma.' She cast a sultry look up at Max. A muscle was beating steadily in his cheek. 'I met Max here in the market and told him what a disastrous time we're having, and he's very kindly going to give us a lift in his car.'

She looked around expectantly, evidently waiting for lavish protestations of gratitude. With a superhuman effort, Cairo pulled herself together.

'There's really no need,' she began. Her voice sounded stiff and high, and Max interrupted her smoothly.

'It's no trouble,' he said. He smiled deliberately down at Jasmin and then looked directly at Cairo. He remembered her all right. 'In fact, it'll be a pleasure.'

Cairo's green eyes blazed murder. How dared he? How dared he stand there in front of her and fawn over Jasmin like that? She had never seen him look so fatuous. Look at him, lapping it up! Jealousy clawed so tightly at her heart that she could hardly speak, and Jasmin's eyes narrowed suspiciously at the unguarded expression on her face.

'What do you mean, there's no need?' she asked sharply. 'I'm not squeezing into two cars with everyone else, and that's that! Since you haven't been able to make the proper arrangements, we really don't have any option but to take Max up on his kind offer.'

Cairo had herself under better control now. 'I've just arranged for a third car,' she said frigidly, 'so there'll be plenty of room for everybody. We don't need to bother Mr Falconer.'

'Let me give you a lift anyway, Jasmin,' Max suggested. 'That'll give everyone else more room, and me the pleasure of your company.' He glanced at Cairo. 'I know the way.'

Cairo's fingers tightened round her clipboard and Jasmin preened herself at another easy conquest. 'That would be lovely,' she purred. 'Since this godforsaken place doesn't have a bar, why don't we go and have a coffee while Cairo sorts everything out? It seems to have been an absolute shambles so far.'

She bore Max off into the hotel, leaving Cairo shaking with fury, frustration and searing jealousy. Max, of all people, to be taken in by those obvious, overblown looks!

So much for all his pontification about the desert and not being concerned with appearances!

Unable to bear the prospect of watching Max drool all over Jasmin, she refused to join the others in the cool, and insisted on waiting outside in the pounding heat until the third car arrived. When it eventually turned up, she steeled herself to go inside and get everybody organised.

'I think we're ready to go,' she announced with a brittle smile.

'You all set off, darlings,' drawled Jasmin. 'We'll be along as soon as we can. Max has decided that his jeep isn't good enough for me, so he's going to borrow one with air-conditioning.'

'How touching,' said Cairo between her teeth.

'I don't like the thought of Jasmin getting covered in dust,' Max explained gravely, and she glared at him. It was all right for *her* to get hot and dirty in his rotten jeep!

'I hope you're good at digging,' she said to Jasmin. 'He's got a nasty habit of driving into soft sand.'

Jasmin gave a complacent smile and ran her finger down Max's forearm in a way that made Cairo break out in a cold sweat of sheer hatred. 'Max seems like the kind of man who can deal with things by himself,' she purred.

'I wouldn't dream of asking Jasmin to touch a shovel,' said Max, meeting Cairo's angry green eyes blandly. 'You mustn't worry about your star. I'll look after her.'

'Well, don't be late,' she said curtly, hardly trusting herself to speak. 'There's a lot of money riding on this one day's shooting, and we won't be able to do anything until Jasmin gets there.' Unable to bear the sight of them together any longer, she turned on her heel and walked out before Jasmin had a chance to start throwing her perfect weight around.

As it was, they had to wait forty minutes before Max and Jasmin finally rolled up at the location, and everyone was fretful while they waited for her to arrive. As soon as she appeared, she was whisked off to be made up in one of the tents Cairo had arranged to have set up for some shade.

She was furious to see that Max had gone to the trouble of borrowing a brand-new Range Rover to transport Jasmin in style. No rickety jeep or clouds of dust for her! Sick with misery, Cairo retreated to the shade and sat on a rock, hugging her arms around her as if she was cold. Max found her there as Jasmin posed on the tops of the dunes and between the rocks.

'I hope you're pleased with this farce you've set up?' he said. 'I suppose you prefer the desert with all these people carrying on as if the world begins and ends on celluloid?'

'Not as much as you seem to,' Cairo snapped. 'Jasmin seems to have made quite a conquest! I must say, I'm surprised at you. I'd have thought you'd have gone for the goody-two-shoes, apple-cheeked, squeaky-clean type.'

Max looked down at her, and, although he didn't smile, she had the infuriating feeling that he was amused. 'No,' he said. 'That's not my type at all.'

'Obviously not!' Cairo glared over to where Jasmin was going through her paces in front of the camera. 'It didn't take much to bowl you over, did it? After all you've had to say about women, you go and fall for someone as obvious as Jasmin. You're just as much a fool as everyone else you're usually busy feeling so superior about. If it wasn't so sad, I'd laugh!'

'Who said I'd fallen for Jasmin?' asked Max blandly.

'You made it pretty obvious.' Cairo mimicked Jasmin's husky drawl. '"I've found a gallant knight. Max has decided that his jeep isn't good enough for me". You were lapping it up!'

Max pretended to consider. 'I wouldn't say that.'

'You probably wouldn't, but, for someone who supposedly finds rocks such good company, you were absolutely riveted by her!'

'She's a very beautiful girl,' said Max, as if that explained everything, and Cairo's eyes flashed green fire.

'If you like that cloying, overblown look and the temperament of an egotistical monster!'

Max tipped back his hat and regarded her thoughtfully. 'You aren't jealous, by any chance, are you, Cairo?'

'Jealous?' Cairo jumped up from her rock, managing to achieve a creditable laugh. 'You're welcome to each other!'

'Then aren't you being a little dog-in-the-manger?'

'Jasmin's not interested in you,' she said bitterly. 'She's only interested in herself. She's the type that always has to have a man to hang on to. It doesn't matter who it is. She only picked you up because she thought you could do something for her, and then when she saw that I——' She broke off, appalled. She had so nearly said, 'That I was in love with you.'

Cairo was convinced it was true. Jasmin had read the truth in her face, and, being Jasmin, had decided to put a spoke in her wheel. If Max was going to be in love with anyone, it would be with her. She needn't have bothered, Cairo thought drearily. A dilapidated jeep with the dust blowing in her face had been good enough for *her*.

'That you what?' Max prompted.

'That I knew you,' she amended quickly. 'Don't get too pleased with yourself. You're just a trophy as far as Jasmin's concerned, but she still won't like you so much as looking at another woman while she's around.' She glanced at Jasmin, who was sending dagger looks in their direction. 'In fact, she's not looking at all pleased now. You'd better run along and pant at her feet. She'll want you where she can keep an eye on you, and I don't want to be responsible for spoiling such a beautiful relationship!'

Proud of her self-control, Cairo got up and stalked away towards the tents, but she couldn't resist looking later to see where Max was. There was no sign of him anywhere near Jasmin, who was having her hair sprayed and looking bad-tempered.

Everyone was wilting under the heat, but there was only one more outfit to go. Cairo prowled restlessly around the tents until, bored by the vacuous chatter of the make-up girl, she escaped out to the rocks to put them all behind her. Once away from it all, it was possible to believe that she was alone and that everything was as before. She would wait for Max to appear, and there would be just the two of them here.

Cairo was so wrapped up in her dream that when she heard the sound of someone moving beyond a rocky outcrop, her steps took her over there without thinking. Max was crouched down beside a dramatically layered rock wall, scribbling in a small notebook. Beneath the battered old hat, his head was bent, so she couldn't see his face, but she let her eyes linger on the clean, decisive lines of his body, allowed herself the luxury of remembering how it had felt against hers.

Max looked up without warning, as if the memory had shouted out to him, his light eyes as startling as ever and suddenly intent. Cairo had no chance to wipe the yearning from her face, and as her eyes met his across the stony ground something blazed into life between them.

'Cairo?' Max stepped towards her, and her heart began to pound with a wild, incredulous hope that died as Jasmin's voice behind her cut through the shimmering tension in the air.

'I've been looking for you both everywhere!' The husky drawl had sharpened with suspicion even though Max and Cairo were nowhere near each other. 'Didn't you hear me calling?'

Cairo moistened her lips and wrenched her eyes away from Max. 'No.'

'You must be deaf as well as incompetent!' Jasmin jerked her head in the direction of the shoot. 'We've finished now, so you'd better go and get things organised so we can leave this hell-hole as soon as possible. You're here to do a job, not moon around, and if you want to get paid you'd better start being a bit more efficient than you've been so far. That flea-pit you booked is the worst hotel I've ever stayed in, and we wasted far too much time this morning because you hadn't arranged enough transport.' She threw an alluring look at Max, whose face was carefully expressionless. 'If it hadn't been for Max, I'd have had to squeeze in with everyone else.'

'I don't suppose it would have killed you,' said Cairo wearily, and Jasmin's face hardened.

'I've got a lot of influence with Haydn Deane, and if you're not very careful I'm going to tell them how sullen and uncooperative you've been. If I object, they won't give your pathetic consultancy any more work, and I know that you of all people can't afford to be out of a job.' She paused meaningfully and gave a cruel smile. 'I'd do all I could to keep my consultancy, if I were you, Cairo. With a name like Kingswood, finding a position of trust must be rather difficult nowadays.'

Cairo turned on her heel and walked away. She was shaking. Clearly, Jasmin knew everything about her father, and would enjoy making sure that Max knew too. Cairo's heart seethed with misery and rebellion. She longed to tell Jasmin exactly what she thought of her, but the model's words had been no less than the truth. She *did* have to keep the consultancy going if she wanted any chance at all of paying off those debts, and that meant doing exactly what Jasmin said.

Somehow she got everyone back to Menesset. They were hot and tired, and complained the whole way about the location. Cairo clenched her fists, and tried not to think about what Max and Jasmin were doing in the car which had fallen behind.

'We probably won't see Jasmin until tomorrow morning now,' said the photographer gloomily, echoing her thoughts. 'You know what she's like once she gets her claws into a man. If she misses the flight, Cairo, you'll have to bring her back with you.'

Cairo had planned to fly back the following afternoon, to give her time to pay all the bills and make sure that she had thanked everyone who had helped her. She had been looking forward to a solitary flight, and she didn't think she could bear to sit next to Jasmin, especially not knowing that she had spent the night with Max.

Her heart felt like a cold, heavy stone in her breast, but the weight on it lifted slightly when the Range Rover stopped outside the hotel. Cairo was standing talking to the manager in the dark entrance hall, and she saw Jasmin get out of the car and go round to Max's window. She looked away, unwilling to witness the lingering goodbye kiss that was undoubtedly going on. The sound of the car driving away was one of the sweetest things she had ever heard. At least Jasmin wasn't spending the night with him.

Jasmin, in fact, was looking rather brittle as she came into the hall, and her eyes narrowed as she saw Cairo. 'I told Max about your father's disgrace,' she said spitefully, 'and he looked absolutely appalled. I was amazed he hadn't heard. It's not as if there wasn't enough coverage at the time.'

'No,' said Cairo in a low voice, remembering just what that coverage had meant to her and her father.

'I think he was surprised you hadn't told him,' Jasmin went on inexorably. 'There really isn't any point in trying to hide a scandal like that, you know, Cairo. It will always come out.'

'It will as long as there are people like you around,' Cairo agreed quietly.

Jasmin shook back her long, glorious black hair. 'I don't know what I'd have done without him today! I said I was sure you'd want to thank him tomorrow, but he said he had to go off somewhere now, so there isn't any point in you looking for him.'

'I'm sure you've thanked him more than adequately,' Cairo said evenly, and turned deliberately back to the manager. Her eyes were glassy, but she wouldn't give Jasmin the satisfaction of knowing how much she had hurt her.

Max's message was clear enough. He didn't want to see her again, and now she wouldn't even have the chance to say goodbye.

CHAPTER TEN

CAIRO lay on the lumpy bed and stared at a crack in the ceiling. When the scandal first broke around her father, she had been shocked and distressed, but there had been nothing like this numbing sense of misery. Then, she had had her father to fight for and plan with. She had been desperately unhappy the last time she had left Menesset, too, but at least she had known she would be coming back, and there had always been that secret hope that she would see Max again. Now, she didn't even have that. He had gone, without even saying goodbye.

It was a relief to put the group on the plane the next morning and stop smiling. Jasmin's taunting beauty was a constant reminder of the last time she had seen Max, and the mere sight of her lacerated Cairo with bitter jealousy. Bearing the model's comments about future jobs in mind, Cairo had tried to appear cheerful and efficient as she ushered everyone through the airport formalities, but the effort left her feeling drained.

She was going to have to get used to it, she realised bleakly. She had a lifetime to get through without Max.

Back in Menesset, she paid off the drivers and added a generous tip. They deserved it after putting up with that lot, Cairo thought. The constant complaints and negative attitudes of her compatriots towards the desert had been embarrassing. She hated to think that she had been like that. No wonder Max had despised her.

She spent the morning being diplomatic and thanking every official she could find at his desk, though why she was thanking them for making her wade through reams of red tape and complicated bureaucratic procedures before they would stamp a permit or tell her she was in the wrong office she wasn't quite sure.

She made a point of thanking everybody in the hotel too. Jasmin had not been the only one to make no secret of her opinion of the facilities, and Cairo had been humbled by the staff's gentle courtesy in the face of such rudeness. She managed to keep smiling throughout the manager's long speech of appreciation, but escaped at last to carry her bag down to the market square where the taxis waited in the shade of the tamarisk trees.

Whenever she had seen them before, there had been a whole fleet of cars parked together, their drivers leaning against the bonnets and smoking cigarettes as they gossiped, or sleeping sprawled across the front seat. Cairo had always wondered how on earth they all made a living. Apart from the airport and the camp, there wasn't anywhere else to go in a taxi.

That afternoon, only two taxis sat in the shade. Both drivers sat in the front car, smoking, and watched Cairo's approach with appreciative eyes.

She put down her bag and bent to speak through the window, but when she asked in French if they would take her to the airport, the men shook their heads. Wondering if they'd misunderstood, she asked again, and when this met with no more response was reduced to spreading her arms and making aeroplane noises.

'You seem to be having some difficulty.' Max's cool voice spoke behind her and she swung round, arms still outstretched. He was wearing his hat and his old khaki shirt, and the light eyes were unmistakably amused as they surveyed her.

For a moment, Cairo simply stared at him, while her eyes drank him in, until she noticed the amusement in his eyes deepen and realised suddenly that her arms were still imitating wings. She dropped them hastily, struggling to control the heart that was battering uncomfortably against her ribs. His obvious amusement annoyed her. Here she was, breaking her heart over him, and all he could do was laugh at her!

'I thought you'd gone,' she said rudely.

'Did you?' Max didn't sound very concerned.

'You know I did. Don't worry, Jasmin passed on your message very clearly. You were going away and didn't want me bothering you.' Cairo's chin came up. 'Not that I had any intention of trying to find you!'

'Did Jasmin tell you I asked her to give you that message?' asked Max, his eyes still glinting infuriatingly.

What was so funny? wondered Cairo bitterly. 'No,' she said. 'But it was painfully obvious.'

'I see.' Max didn't even bother to deny it. He glanced down at Cairo's bag. 'It looks as if you're leaving.'

'I'm trying to,' she said with a vengeful look at the taxi drivers. 'My plane leaves in an hour and a half, and I've got to get out to the airport, but they don't seem to want to understand.'

'Would you like me to talk to them for you?' he asked, evidently determined to make sure that nothing stood in the way of her leaving.

Cairo's pride wouldn't let her admit how much his attitude hurt, not even to herself. It was agony to be near him and not be able to touch him. Having longed to see him just once more, she was now desperate to leave, terrified of giving in and simply throwing herself at his feet. She didn't want Max to remember her like that.

'Thank you,' she said stiffly.

He plunged into rapid, gesticulating Arabic with the two men. There seemed to be a lot of laughter involved, Cairo thought suspiciously. Surely it didn't take this long just to tell one of them to take her to the airport?

Max turned to her at last. 'This one can't go because he's waiting for his cousin, and the other wants to eat in half an hour and if he goes to the airport he'll be late back.'

'Great!' Cairo pushed her hair behind her ears and sighed. 'You'd think they'd be grateful for some business, wouldn't you? It's not as if they've been rushed off their feet all day. How am I supposed to get to the airport?'

'I'll take you if you like,' Max offered. 'I'm going out that way anyway.'

'Thank you, but you did enough for Haydn Deane yesterday,' Cairo refused with cold dignity. 'I'm sure I'll be able to find someone to take me.'

The suspicion that he was making fun of her was too much to bear, and she turned quickly to walk away before he saw how desperately hurt she was. *His* heart wasn't breaking at the prospect of never seeing her again, and she clung to her pride as she walked stiff-backed down the wide shady street. Pride was all she had left.

Cairo walked around the market place, and up and down the neighbouring streets, but the taxis had all mysteriously vanished. At this rate she would miss her plane, she thought, glancing worriedly at her watch.

The Range Rover slid to a stop beside her. 'You might as well get in,' said Max, leaning across to open the passenger door.

Cairo bit her lip and looked up and down the road in the desperate hope that a taxi might suddenly materialise, but there was only a donkey flickering its ears in the shade, and two women shrouded in black, chattering as they headed towards the market place.

She didn't have any choice. Climbing reluctantly into the car, Cairo sat rigidly upright. It was as if Max had determined to make things difficult for her, to taunt her with his presence and the mocking amusement in his eyes, and she clutched her hands together in her lap. All she wanted now was to go home; somehow she would have to get through this trip with him, and then it would be over, and she would be able to cry.

The air-conditioning was deliciously cool and the upholstery luxurious compared to the wreck Max had taken her in before. 'What's wrong with your jeep?' she asked after a moment's silence, hoping her voice wouldn't quaver with the threat of tears.

'The jeep's fine,' Max said.

'Then why are you borrowing this again? Or did Jasmin give you a taste for luxury?'

'It's not borrowed. It's mine.'

'Yours?' Cairo turned to stare at him, tears momentarily forgotten in the slow dawning of outrage. 'Do you mean to say,' she said very carefully, 'that you took me out in that crummy old jeep and let me get covered in sand when all the time we could have been driving in this?'

The crease at the corner of Max's mouth deepened in amusement. 'I'm afraid so.'

'Whereas only this was good enough for Jasmin!' Cairo was too angry to remember that she had been determined not to show him how hurt she had been.

'You see, Jasmin's not like you,' Max said, as if that explained everything.

'I suppose I should be honoured that I'm being driven in the same car as Jasmin,' she snapped. 'Or is that just because you're anxious to make sure that I actually leave?'

'Not as anxious as you seem to be to go.' He turned his head to look at her, his eyes very light. 'Do you really want to?'

Cairo's jaw was clenched, her green eyes ablaze. 'I can't wait!'

'That's a shame,' said Max with no trace of regret, and swung the wheel so that the car veered off the road and raced off at a tangent to the tarmac. 'I'm afraid you're just going to have to wait!'

'What are you doing?' cried Cairo, startled and clinging to dashboard, as the car rocked over the ridges in the sand. 'I'll miss my plane!'

'You will,' Max agreed cheerfully, changing gear. In their wake, the dust rose like a swirling cloud as they bowled across the sand.

Cairo pressed her lips together. 'This isn't funny, Max. Take me to the airport at once!'

'Why?'

'*Why*? Because I want to catch my plane, of course!'

'Well, I want to talk to you,' said Max firmly. 'If you still want to get on the plane tomorrow, I'll take you to the airport and buy you a new ticket. That's fair, isn't it?'

'But Max, this is madness! Where are you going?'

'To the pool.' He glanced at her. 'You remember the pool, don't you, Cairo?'

Cairo looked away. Of course she remembered. Why was he taunting her like this? 'I don't see why you have to kidnap me,' she said defiantly. 'You had plenty of opportunity to talk to me yesterday if you wanted to.'

'I couldn't talk to you with all those ghastly people around.'

'I didn't notice you thinking that Jasmin was ghastly,' Cairo said, unable to disguise her bitterness. 'In fact, you gave a very good impression of being besotted!'

'Did I?' Max sounded pleased. 'I must be a better actor than I thought.'

There was a silence while Cairo assimilated this. 'Actor?' she echoed cautiously at last.

'You don't really think I'd be taken in by someone like Jasmin, do you?' he said with an amused look.

'But...I don't understand,' Cairo said helplessly. 'Why go through all that pretence?'

'To make you jealous, of course.' Max put his foot on the brake and changed down as the car cruised to a stop. 'I thought it was obvious.'

He turned off the engine, and the silence enveloped them. They sat in the car, marooned in a vast expanse of sand. Cairo could have turned in a complete circle and seen nothing but horizon, broken only by the occasional outcrop of rock in the distance that was no more than a smudge shimmering in the heat. Above them, the sky was a deep, unrelenting blue.

'No,' she said slowly, hardly daring to hope. 'It wasn't obvious.'

Max sat forward and leant his arms on the steering-wheel. The lurking amusement had vanished, leaving him suddenly serious and somehow uncertain. He didn't look at Cairo. 'I missed you when you left,' he said. 'I told myself I was glad you had gone. I told myself you didn't belong here and that Piers was welcome to you, but I still missed you.' He paused, his eyes fixed on the flat, limitless horizon. 'The desert seemed empty without you.'

Cairo couldn't speak. She could only sit and watch his profile, hardly daring to let herself hope again, while the cold claws of misery began to release themselves very cautiously from her heart.

'Of course, you'd made it very clear that your job was more important to you than I was,' he went on after a moment. 'I'd hoped that you were beginning to like the desert, and I was very bitter when it seemed that you couldn't wait to get back to London after that night we spent together at the pool. I decided I'd been a fool to even think that you had changed. When I left you at the camp, I just wanted to forget about you, but I couldn't. I kept turning round expecting to see you. I wanted to hear your voice and see you smile. I wanted to touch you.' His voice was very low. 'I wouldn't even have minded watching you fuss around in your make-up bag!'

Cairo found her voice at last as a smile trembled on her lips. 'I can't believe you missed that!'

'It was part of you,' said Max. 'Of course I missed it.' Still leaning on the wheel, he turned his head to look at her. 'Eventually, I just gave in. I knew you'd be coming back with the shoot, and as I know all the officials in Menesset it was easy to find out when you were arriving. I hung around the town, just hoping to see you. As soon as I saw Jasmin, I knew she must be part of your group, so I attached myself to her. I wasn't sure if you'd want to see me, but I thought if I could just tag along with everyone I'd be bound to get the chance to talk to you.'

'But why did you make such a fuss of Jasmin?' Cairo burst out. 'You must have known what I thought!'

'It only occurred to me when I saw the look on your face when you saw us together.' Max half smiled. 'You've got a very expressive face, Cairo, and if looks could kill, Jasmin would have disintegrated on the spot. That's when I began to hope. You wouldn't have been that jealous if I hadn't meant anything to you, so I played up to Jasmin—a little too successfully! She wouldn't leave me alone.

'In the end, I told her I had some urgent work to do and wouldn't be able to stay in Menesset to see her that night. The message you thought I'd sent you was the only way I could think of to get rid of her! She did tell me that you would be staying behind until the later flight, though, so I decided I would just wait until everyone else had gone.'

Cairo looked down at her hands. 'Did she also tell you about my father?' she asked quietly. She couldn't let herself be happy until she was sure that he knew everything.

'Yes, she did.' Max had still made no move to touch her. 'Why didn't you tell me?' His voice was warm and gentle, and Cairo felt sudden tears sting her eyes.

'I knew how you felt about corruption,' she said with difficulty, twisting her fingers together. She always found it hard to talk about the shame she had felt when she had first discovered what her father had been doing. 'My father was guilty of that, and now he's suffering the consequences, but I didn't think you'd have any sympathy with him. To you he'd just be a typical example of city dishonesty, but for me he's still the loving, generous father he always was.'

'Jasmin said you were working to pay off his debts,' said Max. 'Is that why you were so desperate to make this job a success?'

Cairo nodded. 'I can't let my father down. I know that he only did what he did so that he could carry on spoiling me, and I feel so responsible,' she whispered in a sudden rush of anguish. 'You were always telling me how spoilt I was, and I thought that if you knew just what had made all the spoiling possible you would just despise me even more.'

Max reached out and touched her hair very lightly. 'I would never despise loyalty, Cairo.'

'Jasmin said you looked appalled when she told you about my father,' she said, unable to disguise her bitterness.

'I did, but it was only because I realised how much I'd misjudged you. I was doing what I always accused you of doing, and judging by appearances. You carry this air of glamour around with you, Cairo. It doesn't matter what you wear or what you're doing.' Max hesitated, letting his hands slide around the steering-wheel.

'Because you were beautiful and self-assured, I thought you would be as vain and superficial as my mother, but I should have known better. I'd had ample opportunity to see how brave and funny you were, and when Jasmin told me about your father I realised how loyal you were too. It wasn't a good feeling to know just how wrong I'd been about you.' His gaze rested on her face. 'Your father is a very lucky man. I envy him.'

'You do?' Her eyes were huge and puzzled.

'You love him very much, don't you?'

'Yes,' she said. 'Yes, I do.'

Max looked back towards the horizon. 'I haven't given you any reason to love *me*. I haven't spoilt you and cosseted you like your father. I've shouted at you and criticised you and deliberately made things hard for you in the hope that you'd give up and prove to me that you were just like all the city girls I'd ever met who were all froth and no substance. But you never gave up. You just gritted your teeth and climbed up to that plateau, and walked through the locusts, and dug out the jeep, and the more gutsy and determined you were, the more I fell in love with you.' He paused. 'I didn't want to fall in love with you, Cairo. I tried my very hardest not to. You were like a thorn in my side. Everything about you seemed designed to remind me that you were probably as spoilt and selfish and superficial as my mother. I remembered you perfectly well from that party. I'd noticed you all evening, and I didn't like the fact that I could find a girl like you attractive. It was exactly the same when you turned up in the desert, absolutely determined to have your own way. I was equally determined not to like you, but I couldn't get the thought of kissing you out of my mind. Every night I had to hold you in my arms and not touch you, and it made me very bad-tempered!'

'Didn't you ever wonder why *I* was so cross?' Cairo asked, a glow just starting in her eyes, and Max shook his head slowly.

'No. I'd given you every reason to hate me, and I thought you did. At the guelta... I wondered, but you seemed so determined to finish the job and go home, I thought you couldn't wait to leave, so I didn't even try. And after that night at the pool, when I asked you to stay and you wouldn't, I decided I must have been wrong in thinking that it had meant as much to you as it had to me. I didn't know about your father then, or why you felt you had to go back.'

'You only asked me to stay for one more day,' Cairo said. 'I couldn't let everyone down just for one day, no matter how much I wanted to stay.'

'I didn't want to frighten you with talk of forever,' he explained. 'I can't offer you the kind of life you're used to, Cairo. I'm just not that kind of man. I felt I couldn't ask you to give up everything to stay here with me in the desert. It was only when I saw the way you looked at me yesterday that I thought I would ask you anyway. You said once that you had never got married because you were waiting for a man who really loved you...' He trailed off. Cairo had never seen him so unsure of himself.

Her heart was so full that for a moment she couldn't say anything, and Max misinterpreted her silence. 'It's a lot to ask, I know,' he said with a show of briskness, and glanced at his watch. 'I do understand. I just wanted you to know how I felt.' He reached for the ignition key. 'I'll take you to the airport now. There's still just time to catch your plane.'

Cairo couldn't believe that he could be so obtuse. 'Max?' she said, and something in her voice made his fingers fall from the key. He straightened slowly and turned to face her. His face was taut, but the grey-green eyes were blazing with sudden hope.

'Yes?'

For a moment Cairo just looked at him, wondering how she could begin to explain, then she leant forward and kissed him very gently on the corner of his mouth. 'I don't want to catch the plane,' she said simply. 'I never did.'

The look in his eyes made her heart turn over. 'You mean you'll stay?'

'Yes.'

'You love me?'

Cairo smiled at last, a warm, radiant smile that lit up her face and was reflected in his eyes. 'Desperately,' she admitted, and the next instant she was in his arms, and he was kissing her with deep, hungry kisses. She melted against him as joy exploded in her heart, holding his neck between her hands so that she could kiss him back.

They broke apart at last, breathless and giddy with happiness. 'You *do* love me,' said Max, as if he was only just convinced, covering her face with kisses.

'I told you I did,' Cairo managed with difficulty.

'And you'll marry me? Soon?'

'Yes ... yes,' she gasped, drunk with the delight of his mouth against hers and the incredible, wonderful, exhilarating knowledge that he loved her after all.

'I've been so miserable without you,' she said, leaning her head against his shoulder at last. 'I couldn't bear

184 OASIS OF THE HEART

the thought of leaving, without even saying goodbye.'
In the distance, she watched a plane climb into the blue
sky above the airport. The sun glinted silver on its wings
as it banked sharply and headed north.

'I might have been on that if I had managed to find
a taxi,' she said with a shudder as the realisation hit her.
'Oh, Max, I might never have seen you again!'

'You don't think I left it to chance, do you?' said Max,
tightening his arms around her. 'I paid every single taxi
driver in Menesset the return fare to the airport to refuse
to take you.'

Cairo pulled slightly away from him, scandalised.
'Max! How extravagant!'

'I thought you were worth it,' said Max, and kissed
her again. 'Anyway, I can afford it. If the worst came
to the worst, I thought I might persuade you to marry
me for my money! I've got more of the stuff than I know
what to do with.'

'It's a pity you didn't spend it keeping that jeep in
better condition,' Cairo pretended to scold.

Max looked defensive. 'She's normally very reliable,'
he said, but had the grace to laugh when Cairo did. 'It
was just unfortunate that she broke down that day. I
wished I'd taken this car after all.'

'Why didn't you? It would have been a lot more
comfortable!'

'Sheer bloody-mindedness,' he said, his hands tightening against her. 'You'd spent all night flirting with
Bruce, remember. I was beside myself with jealousy and
determined to make you suffer for it!'

'I certainly did that!' said Cairo with feeling, remembering what it had been like digging out the jeep.

Max laughed. 'I was a pig to you that day. I'm sorry.'
He took her hand and pressed a kiss into her palm,
curling her fingers over as if to keep it there. 'I'll spend
the rest of my life making it up to you,' he promised
and she sighed with happiness.

'You made it up to me that night,' she reminded him with a wicked smile, and his hands tightened against her.

'Exactly,' he said.

'It wasn't just that day either,' Cairo pointed out, teasing. 'You were vile to me most of the time on the plateau, and as for that performance with Jasmin...well! You'll have to work very hard to make all that up!'

Max grinned. 'I'll make a start as soon as we get to the pool.'

'Promises, promises!'

He kissed her once, hard, and released her. 'If we don't get a move-on, we won't get to the pool at all tonight,' he told her, and Cairo slid reluctantly back to her side of the seat as he set the car moving once more.

The pool was just as she had remembered it, a quiet, cool green. Cairo held Max's hand as she stood looking down into its clear depths and thought that her heart would burst with happiness. She wanted to go for a swim straight away, but the light was draining rapidly from the sky and Max insisted on setting up the camp first.

'We don't want to be blundering around in the dark,' he said, and pulled her against him. 'We've got better things to do then. Let's be sensible now.'

'I haven't got a sleeping mat,' Cairo said, muffled against his shoulder, as she was struck by the sudden thought. 'I knew we'd be staying in a hotel, so I didn't bring anything like that with me this time.'

'I've got an extra one,' said Max casually. Cairo was inclined to think that it was fortunate until she saw him unpack two mugs and two plates.

'You were very sure of me,' she accused him.

Max stood up and took her hands. His face was serious. 'I wasn't sure at all, Cairo. I just hoped, but all I had to go on was that one blazing look you sent Jasmin. I wasn't nearly as confident as I pretended to be, and I would have taken you on to the airport straight away if that's what you'd wanted.' His fingers tightened around hers. 'I don't like to think about what a lonely night this would have been if you'd decided you didn't want to stay.'

'I'll never decide that,' said Cairo quietly. 'But I will have to go home some time, Max. I've still got my father to think about.'

'We'll go back together,' he promised. 'We'll pay off your father's debts and you can tell Piers he'll have to start looking for a new partner. If he's got any sense, he'll include Joanna in his schemes. She doesn't need to work, but having a job like that might give her some of the confidence she needs. She could also keep an eye on Piers that way!'

Cairo looked at him in surprise. 'You mean you don't mind about Piers any more?'

'I don't mind nearly as much as I did when I thought he might be involved with you,' Max confessed. 'You were right about me being too protective of Joanna. I've looked after her since I was nine, and I suppose I got used to it, but it might have been better if I'd let her look after herself a bit more.'

'I don't think the poor girl will get much chance to be independent,' said Cairo drily. 'Piers is determined to look after her too!'

'He wrote to me,' Max said unexpectedly. 'He said he understood that I might not be too keen on the idea of him marrying my sister, but that he loved her and wouldn't rush her into anything before he'd proved that he'd made a success of his business.' Max made a disgusted noise. 'He sounds a bit too smarmy for my liking, but if Joanna's determined to have him I suppose I'll have to make the best of it.' He sighed. 'He even had the cheek to finish by saying that he gathered I'd met his partner, Miss Kingswood, and any help I could give her on her forthcoming trip to Shofrar would be very much appreciated!'

She laughed. 'I didn't tell him quite how much you'd done for us already,' she offered as an excuse for Piers.

'For *you*,' Max corrected, catching her against him. 'How are *you* going to show me your appreciation?'

Cairo slipped her arms around him and ran her fingers down his spine. 'I'll think of something,' she promised in a silky voice, kissing his throat, and Max smiled as he began unbuttoning her shirt.

'Start thinking now,' he suggested.

Discarding clothes as they went, he drew her over to the sleeping mats. 'I thought we were supposed to be being sensible and setting up the camp?' Cairo reminded him, already breathless beneath the devastating exploration of his hands.

Max pulled her down beside him, and bent his head to find her mouth with his own. 'It can wait,' he said.

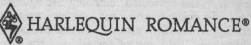

HARLEQUIN ROMANCE®

brings you:

Penny Sullivan moves away to start a new life when her love affair with Reid Branden ends in bitterness—but her young niece unwittingly brings them back together again. Will Penny and Reid's love blossom again—or will the past continue to haunt them?

#3366—P.S. I LOVE YOU by Valerie Parv
June's *Sealed with a Kiss* title

Available wherever Harlequin Books are sold.

In coming months, watch for these exciting
Sealed with a Kiss titles:

July: #3369—*Wanted: Wife and Mother*
by Barbara McMahon
August: #3373—*The Best for Last*
by Stephanie Howard
September: #3378—*Angels Do Have Wings*
by Helen Brooks

Harlequin Romance—Dare to Dream

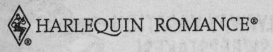

HARLEQUIN ROMANCE®

celebrates

Join us in June for *Family Ties!*

Family...what does it bring to mind? The trials and pleasures of children and grandchildren, loving parents and close bonds with brothers and sisters—that special joy a close family can bring. Whatever meaning it has for you, we know you'll enjoy these heartwarming love stories in which we celebrate family—and in which you can meet some fascinating members of our heroes' and heroines' families.

It all begins with...

#3365 *Simply the Best*
by Catherine Spencer

ANNOUNCING THE

FLYAWAY VACATION SWEEPSTAKES!

This month's destination:

Beautiful SAN FRANCISCO!

This month, as a special surprise, we're offering an exciting FREE VACATION!

Think how much fun it would be to visit San Francisco "on us"! You could ride cable cars, visit Chinatown, see the Golden Gate Bridge and dine in some of the finest restaurants in America!

The facing page contains two Entry Coupons (as does every book you received this shipment). Complete and return *all* the entry coupons; **the more times you enter, the better your chances of winning!**

Then keep your fingers crossed, because you'll find out by June 15, 1995 if you're the winner! If you are, here's what you'll get:

- • Round-trip airfare for two to beautiful San Francisco!
- • 4 days/3 nights at a first-class hotel!
- • $500.00 pocket money for meals and sightseeing!

Remember: The more times you enter, the better your chances of winning!*

VSF KAL

FLYAWAY VACATION
SWEEPSTAKES
OFFICIAL ENTRY COUPON

This entry must be received by: MAY 30, 1995
This month's winner will be notified by: JUNE 15, 1995
Trip must be taken between: JULY 30, 1995-JULY 30, 1996

YES, I want to win the San Francisco vacation for two. I understand the prize includes round-trip airfare, first-class hotel and $500.00 spending money. Please let me know if I'm the winner!

Name_____

Address _____ Apt. _____

City   State/Prov.   Zip/Postal Code

Account #_____

Return entry with invoice in reply envelope.

© 1995 HARLEQUIN ENTERPRISES LTD.   CSF KAL

FLYAWAY VACATION
SWEEPSTAKES
OFFICIAL ENTRY COUPON

This entry must be received by: MAY 30, 1995
This month's winner will be notified by: JUNE 15, 1995
Trip must be taken between: JULY 30, 1995-JULY 30, 1996

YES, I want to win the San Francisco vacation for two. I understand the prize includes round-trip airfare, first-class hotel and $500.00 spending money. Please let me know if I'm the winner!

Name_____

Address _____ Apt. _____

City   State/Prov.   Zip/Postal Code

Account #_____

Return entry with invoice in reply envelope.

© 1995 HARLEQUIN ENTERPRISES LTD.   CSF KAL

OFFICIAL RULES

FLYAWAY VACATION SWEEPSTAKES 3449
NO PURCHASE OR OBLIGATION NECESSARY

Three Harlequin Reader Service 1995 shipments will contain respectively, coupons for entry into three different prize drawings, one for a trip for two to San Francisco, another for a trip for two to Las Vegas and the third for a trip for two to Orlando, Florida. To enter any drawing using an Entry Coupon, simply complete and mail according to directions.

There is no obligation to continue using the Reader Service to enter and be eligible for any prize drawing. You may also enter any drawing by hand printing the words "Flyaway Vacation," your name and address on a 3"x5" card and the destination of the prize you wish that entry to be considered for (i.e., San Francisco trip, Las Vegas trip or Orlando trip). Send your 3"x5" entries via first-class mail (limit: one entry per envelope) to: Flyaway Vacation Sweepstakes 3449, c/o Prize Destination you wish that entry to be considered for, P.O. Box 1315, Buffalo, NY 14269-1315, USA or P.O. Box 610, Fort Erie, Ontario L2A 5X3, Canada.

To be eligible for the San Francisco trip, entries must be received by 5/30/95; for the Las Vegas trip, 7/30/95; and for the Orlando trip, 9/30/95.

Winners will be determined in random drawings conducted under the supervision of D.L. Blair, Inc., an independent judging organization whose decisions are final, from among all eligible entries received for that drawing. San Francisco trip prize includes round-trip airfare for two, 4-day/3-night weekend accommodations at a first-class hotel, and $500 in cash (trip must be taken between 7/30/95—7/30/96, approximate prize value—$3,500); Las Vegas trip includes round-trip airfare for two, 4-day/3-night weekend accommodations at a first-class hotel, and $500 in cash (trip must be taken between 9/30/95—9/30/96, approximate prize value—$3,500); Orlando trip includes round-trip airfare for two, 4-day/3-night weekend accommodations at a first-class hotel, and $500 in cash (trip must be taken between 11/30/95—11/30/96, approximate prize value—$3,500). All travelers must sign and return a Release of Liability prior to travel. Hotel accommodations and flights are subject to accommodation and schedule availability. Sweepstakes open to residents of the U.S. (except Puerto Rico) and Canada, 18 years of age or older. Employees and immediate family members of Harlequin Enterprises, Ltd., D.L. Blair, Inc., their affiliates, subsidiaries and all other agencies, entities and persons connected with the use, marketing or conduct of this sweepstakes are not eligible. Odds of winning a prize are dependent upon the number of eligible entries received for that drawing. Prize drawing and winner notification for each drawing will occur no later than 15 days after deadline for entry eligibility for that drawing. Limit: one prize to an individual, family or organization. All applicable laws and regulations apply. Sweepstakes offer void wherever prohibited by law. Any litigation within the province of Quebec respecting the conduct and awarding of the prizes in this sweepstakes must be submitted to the Regies des loteries et Courses du Quebec. In order to win a prize, residents of Canada will be required to correctly answer a time-limited arithmetical skill-testing question. Value of prizes are in U.S. currency.

Winners will be obligated to sign and return an Affidavit of Eligibility within 30 days of notification. In the event of noncompliance within this time period, prize may not be awarded. If any prize or prize notification is returned as undeliverable, that prize will not be awarded. By acceptance of a prize, winner consents to use of his/her name, photograph or other likeness for purposes of advertising, trade and promotion on behalf of Harlequin Enterprises, Ltd., without further compensation, unless prohibited by law.

For the names of prizewinners (available after 12/31/95), send a self-addressed, stamped envelope to: Flyaway Vacation Sweepstakes 3449 Winners, P.O. Box 4200, Blair, NE 68009.

RVC KAL